Rubies in the Snow

Rubies in the Snow

Kate Hubbard

✳ SHORT BOOKS

First published in 2006 by
Short Books
3A Exmouth House
Pine Street
EC1R 0JH

10 9 8 7 6 5 4 3 2
Copyright ©
Kate Hubbard 2006

Illustration copyright © Emily Fox
A CIP catalogue record for this book
is available from the British Library.

ISBN 1–904977–73–1
[978-1-904977-73-5]

Printed in the UK by CPI Bookmarque, Croydon, CR0 4TD

For Maud Craigie

Cast your mind back, to the early years of the 20th century. To Russia. An endless country of icy wastes and dusty plains, of silvery birch trees and black earth. A country of extremes. Of unimaginable wealth and unspeakable poverty. Of excess and hunger. Of culture and cruelty. A country ruled for nearly 300 years by one family, long accustomed to power and privilege – the Romanovs. And born into that family is a girl, an ordinary sort of girl in many respects, but one swept up by extraordinary circumstances. Accompany her as her world fragments and shatters...

Rubies in the Snow is a work of fiction, inspired by the life of Anastasia Nicolaevna, youngest daughter of Russia's last Tsar. The main characters are real; the facts are true.

<hr/>

CAST OF CHARACTERS

Nicholas II – Tsar of Russia
Alexandra Feodorovna – the Tsarina
Grand Duchess Olga – daughters of Nicholas and Alexandra
Grand Duchess Tatiana
Grand Duchess Marie
Grand Duchess Anastasia
Alexis – the Tsarevich

<hr/>

Alexander Avdeev – head of the guards at Ekaterinburg
Alexander Kerensky – Prime Minister of the Provisional Government
Alexander Nikolsky – deputy commissar at Tobolsk
Andrei Vasilievich Shuvalov – wounded officer in Anastasia's hospital
Ania Vyrubova – the Tsarina's closest friend
Aunt Ella (Grand Duchess Elizabeth) – the Tsarina's sister
Aunt Olga (Grand Duchess Olga) – the Tsar's sister
Colonel Kobylinsky – Commander of the Guard at Tsarskoe Selo
Count Benckendorff – Grand Marshal of the imperial court
Count Fredericks – Chief Minister at the imperial court
Countess Hendrikov – lady-in-waiting to the Tsarina
Dr Botkin – court doctor
Fat Orlov (Prince Vladimir Orlov) – official at the imperial court

Grand Duke Dmitri Pavlovich – son of Grand Duke Pavel the Tsar's uncle

Grandmama (Marie Feodorovna, Dowager Empress) – the Tsar's mother

Igor Leontich – soldier in the 4th Regiment at Tobolsk

Irina (Grand Duchess Irina) – daughter of the Tsar's sister Xenia

Ivan Ivanovich – soldier in the 4th Regiment at Tobolsk

Ivan Mikhailovich Kharitonov – the imperial family's cook

Ivan Petrovich – wounded soldier in Anastasia's hospital

Jacob Yurovsky – member of the Bolshevik Secret Police

Lenka (Leonid Ivanovich Sednev) – footman to the Grand Duchesses

Lili Dehn – friend of the Tsarina

Maria Pavlovna – daughter of Grand Duke Pavel

Monsieur Gilliard – Alexis's tutor

Mr Gibbes – English tutor

Nyuta (Anna Stefanova Demidova) – the Tsarina's maid

Orchie (Miss Orchard) – the Tsarina's old governess

Our Friend (Grigory Rasputin) – a starets or Man of God

Prince Felix Yusupov – Irina's husband

Pyotr Vasilievich Petrov – literature tutor

Shura – Anastasia's maid

Sovanna (Sophia Ivanovna Tyutcheva) – governess to the Grand Duchesses

Trina (Mademoiselle Schneider) – governess to the Grand Duchesses

Uncle Misha (Grand Duke Michael) – the Tsar's brother

Uncle Willy (William II) – the German Kaiser

Vasily Pankratov – commissar in charge of the imperial family at Tobolsk

Vasili Vasilevich Yakovlev – Bolshevik commissar

1911

⁂

June 18th, Tsarskoe Selo

Today is my birthday. I'm ten. It's also the first day of this diary, a present from Papa and Mama. My name is Anastasia Nicolaevna. Well, in fact my full name is Grand Duchess Anastasia Nicolaevna, but I don't like the Grand Duchess part. Sometimes I'm just called 'the imp'.

I have three sisters – Olga is seventeen, Tatiana is fourteen and Marie is twelve. And then there's Alexis, my brother – he's seven and he's the Tsarevich because Papa is the Tsar. Papa says that diaries are a good habit and he writes his every night before going to bed and Mama says that Great Granny, who was Queen Victoria of England, kept a diary every day of her life and besides it should help with my spelling, which is atrocious.

My other presents – a drawing book, watercolour paints, a tennis racket and a photograph album.

June 19th

This is how my day goes (it's nearly always the same) – after breakfast Dr Botkin comes to give us our daily examination, then we have lessons from 9 o'clock till 11, then we walk in the park with Papa for an hour, then there's another lesson before luncheon. After luncheon we go outside for exercise till 4 o'clock, then we have tea with Papa and Mama, then more lessons, or piano practice or sewing until dinner at 8 o'clock. After dinner Alexis goes to bed and we girls do embroidery while Papa reads to us. I go to bed at 9.30. And I haven't mentioned church and confession. So you can see I'm extremely busy – I hardly have a single minute to write this!

June 21st

I'm going to describe our home (actually it's practice for my composition for Mr Gibbes, who teaches us English). We live in the Alexander Palace at Tsarskoe Selo. It's yellow and white and it was built by Papa's great great great grandmother, Catherine the Great, who was Empress of Russia more than 100 years ago. There's an enormous park all around, so big that you can walk for hours and not get to the edge. Our Cossacks ride around outside the railings all day and all night.

In our wing of the palace Papa and Mama's rooms are downstairs and us children are above. There's a new elevator so Mama doesn't have to use the stairs. Olga and Tatiana share a room and Marie and I share another. Alexis has his own. Marie and I have flowery wallpaper with butterflies along the top, which we chose ourselves. I have 29 icons above my bed. That's two more than Marie.

June 23rd

This morning we had lessons on the terrace as it was so hot. We did arithmetic and geography (my worst subjects) with Sovanna, who's our governess. I was very happy when I heard Papa whistling for us to come and join him for our walk. Mama had a headache so she wasn't at luncheon. Father Vasilev – he's our confessor – came into the dining room as usual, to say the blessing in front of the icon. I don't awfully like Father Vasilev – he looks like a great black crow and his voice is all raspy and rusty as if it needs oiling and he goes on and on when you're starving. We had soup and fish. In the afternoon I climbed trees with Alexis, even though he's not supposed to in case he falls and gets ill again. Luckily Mama didn't know.

June 26th

We had tea today with Ania in her little house in the park. Ania is Mama's best friend, though she's quite a lot younger. Mama says she had an 'unfortunate marriage' – her husband wasn't quite right in the head – and now she lives here and we see her all the time. She looks like a potato and she always agrees with everything Mama says. Sometimes I think she's a bit silly, but she's very kind to us.

Our Friend was there too – his real name is Grigory Rasputin, but Mama likes to call him 'Our Friend'. He doesn't look particularly nice – his hair is all long and greasy and his clothes are always dirty – but he's actually a starets (that means a Man of God and we have lots of them in Russia), in fact a special kind of starets. He's also jolly good at telling stories. Today we had the one about the humpbacked horse.

June 27th

Marie and I still have to have cold baths every morning, even though Olga and Tatiana don't any more and Alexis is let off. Cold water is good for us apparently. And we still have camp beds and no pillows, like Papa used to when he was a boy. This morning I got into trouble with Miss Orchard – we call her 'Orchie' – for not making my bed.

In fact I'd tried to make Marie make it for me – often Marie will just do things for you, but this time she wouldn't.

Orchie used to be Mama's governess when she was a little girl in Darmstadt, which is in Germany. Now she's very old so she doesn't actually teach us, she just bosses the other tutors and nannies. I don't see why I have to make my bed, but Mama says that, even though Papa's the Tsar, that's no reason not to be able to do simple things like making one's own bed. She says that she was taught to make hers by Great Granny and she was very shocked when she came to Russia and realised that Russian ladies didn't know how.

Orchie and Mama think that one should have occupations for every moment of the day and Orchie's always saying 'idle hands make mischief'.

June 30th

Yesterday we had a fancy-dress party. I went as a chimney sweep. This morning I went to my English lesson with Mr Gibbes with my face still all blackened with coal dust and with my gold ladder (for climbing chimneys). Mr Gibbes looked a bit surprised, but he didn't say anything – he just asked me to read. Then Mama and my sisters came in and Mama screamed and said 'Go and wash at once, Anastasia!' So I did and Mr Gibbes went on with the lesson. I kept my ladder with me though. This evening we walked to Znamenia, our favourite church, for mass.

July 1st

The first day of the month so I got my pocket money. I get nine dollars every month, but I have to give two dollars to charities. Mama has pains in her legs and her head so she's been lying down all day on her sofa. I sat with her after tea and drew her a picture. Everything in her room is mauve. Personally mauve makes me feel a bit sick, but it's Mama's favourite colour. Her room always smells delicious though, of lilac and lily of the valley. Mama says she loves lilac because it reminds her of Papa and when they were first engaged to be married in Coburg and he used to bring her a big bunch of lilac every morning.

July 3rd

Alexis is a very odd boy. I found him lying on his back in the park looking up at the sky, so I asked him what he was doing and he said, 'I love to lie and watch the clouds moving. Who knows how long I'll be able to do so.' He means because of his illness I suppose. While we were getting ready for bed Our Friend came and said prayers with us.

July 9th

I wish we didn't always have to wear the same dresses and I wish they weren't always white. At least we can choose our sash. Mine is usually blue, my favourite colour. It's boiling hot. This afternoon Tatiana, Marie and I swam in the big lake, around the children's island. Alexis knocked his elbow on the bookshelves in the schoolroom yesterday, and now it's all swollen and purple and bent, which means that it's bleeding inside. He's been in bed all day and Mama is sitting with him.

Just now I found Shura, my maid, talking to Alexis's nanny in the corridor outside Alexis's room. They were saying things like, 'Oh, poor little boy, what a terrible thing, and him being the heir, and they say the doctors can't help him' etc. And suddenly (I couldn't help it) I burst out, 'Don't talk about the Tsarevich like that! There's absolutely nothing the matter with him! You don't know anything!' They both looked very embarrassed and Shura kept apologising, so I forgave her.

July 11th

Mama asked Our Friend to come and see Alexis, because his arm has been hurting terribly. Our Friend sat with him all evening. Then he came into Mama's sitting room and told us that Alexis had fallen asleep and we weren't to worry. Today Alexis is better! Dr Botkin says the bleeding has stopped. It's all because of Our Friend. Mama is smiling again.

July 13th

Aunt Olga came for lunch. She's Papa's youngest sister and she's also my godmother. She was talking to Tatiana in Mama's sitting room and I kept asking her to come and listen to me practising the balalaika and she said, 'Don't be so provoking, Anastasia. Can't you see I'm talking to Tatiana?' while Tatiana kept sighing and rolling her eyes at me in that superior way she has. When I asked Aunt Olga again she gave me a slap, on my cheek. Then she put her hand over her mouth and said, 'Oh Anastasia, I'm so sorry. Please don't cry.' I could feel my face getting hotter and hotter, but I said, 'I absolutely never cry.' Which is nearly true. Later she came and looked at my drawings.

We're going to Livadia, our palace in the Crimea, soon. It's my favourite place in the world – in fact we all love Livadia and Mama says she feels better there than anywhere else.

July 17th, on the train

We've been on our train for nearly two days. Papa and Mama have one carriage and we have another. Papa has a special contraption on his bath to stop the water sloshing out when we're going along.

When we stopped yesterday, for exercise, Tatiana, Marie, Alexis and I (Olga wouldn't come because she wanted to carry on reading her book) borrowed some silver trays from the pantry and tobogganed down a sort of sandy bank. It was nearly as good as snow. Then Fat Orlov – he's one of our court officials – had a go, which was really a very funny sight as he's so fat now that when he sits down he can't see his knees. His legs stuck in the air and we all had to help pull him up when he got to the bottom of the bank.

Ortino, Tatiana's bulldog, snored last night and kept us all awake.

July 20th, Livadia

I think the Crimea is the greenest place I have ever seen and it definitely has the most delicious grapes! Our palace is right on top of the cliffs and it's brand new and all white, like an enormous lump of sugar. Marie and I can see the sea from our beds – in fact you can see the sea from almost every room in the palace.

There are no lessons because it's the holidays – hurrah! This afternoon we walked with Papa in the woods and picked berries and mushrooms. Papa made a little fire and cooked the mushrooms in a pan. Then we ate them. Delicious!

July 22nd

Marie and I practised tennis in our room till Orchie told us to stop.

July 29th

Alexis was extremely naughty at lunch. He went under the table, which he often does, and took off Countess Hendrikov's shoe. Countess Hendrikov is one of Mama's ladies-in-waiting – she's 28 and she's a spinster. Papa told him to put it back on at once, and he did, but he'd put a very squishy strawberry in the toe and she screamed! He wouldn't apologise.

Alexis is quite spoilt – he isn't punished nearly as often as we girls. I think people feel sorry for him because of his illness, or maybe it's just because he's the heir. After lunch Papa took Alexis for a little walk. When I asked him if

Papa had given him a talking-to he said, 'Oh not really, he just said that when I'm tsar I'll have 150 million people looking up to me, so I'd better learn some manners.' It's quite hard to believe that there are 150 million people in Russia.

July 31st

Today we all went to Ai-Todor, which is Aunt Xenia and Uncle Sandro's house, to have tea and play with my cousins. Aunt Xenia is Papa's sister. On the way we drove through little white villages and lots of Tartars – that's what the people who live in the Crimea are called – came out and rode beside us. They have very dark skin and they wear strange clothes – baggy trousers that go in at the ankles and very bright coloured shirts, a bit like people in *The Arabian Nights*.

I've got seven cousins. Irina is the eldest, a little older than Olga. She's very shy and extremely pretty – she's got black hair and great big dark eyes and white, white skin. And then there are six boys, who are generally very badly behaved. They started a big game of 'Catch the Thief', but Mama wouldn't let Alexis join in as they're so rough. I know Mama is just desperate to make sure Alexis doesn't hurt himself, but sometimes I think she treats him too much like a baby. Later, Misha, one of my cousins, asked me what was wrong with Alexis and I had to say 'nothing', because Papa and Mama say we must never talk about it. Then Misha said, 'Well, why's he such a girl then?' I hate Misha.

August 3rd

Marie got a letter from Our Friend. She didn't want me to read it, so I snatched it and she biffed me. It said: 'My dear pearl Marie! Tell me how you talked with the sea, with nature! I miss your simple soul! We will see each other soon! A big kiss.' I wish he'd write to *me*. Went for a long ride with Papa and Tatiana.

August 8th

Sunday. Went to church in the morning and again in the evening. This afternoon I played tennis with Tatiana against Olga and Marie and we won, mostly because Tatiana is so tall and because Marie nearly always misses. She kept saying sorry, which was very annoying and I said, 'Stop being a fat little bow-wow,' and she cried. Marie is always apologising and trying to be nice to everyone, which is why we call her 'bow-wow', because she's like a lapdog. Tatiana is very good at tennis, but she orders you around the whole time.

August 18th

It was very hot today. Mama sat on the terrace with Ania, who looked very fat and red, and Papa took us swimming. While we were jumping in the waves a huge wave came right over us and I went down under and was tumbled around and then I felt my hair being pulled and Papa yanked me up. He said, 'I fished you out by your hair – it's lucky it's so long!' He thought it was better not to tell Mama. I swallowed a lot of sea but I was perfectly alright.

After tea, when we were all sitting on the terrace, Count Fredericks – he's head of Papa's court and Papa calls him 'the Old Man' because he's been with us for ever – came to tell Alexis that some peasants had arrived with a gift for him. They'd walked for three days to get here. When Alexis heard they were waiting, he said, 'Now girls, run away, I have some business to attend to,' in a drawling sort of voice! So we bowed and I said, 'As you wish your Most Gracious and High and Mighty and Worshipful Imperial Majesty.' Alexis's gift was an embroidered coat and pointy leather slippers, which he says he won't wear on any account.

September 2nd

Yesterday there was a ball for Olga's sixteenth birthday (in fact her actual birthday was last year). Olga had her hair put up. She wore a proper ballgown (pink) and her first jewels – a necklace of diamonds and pearls and a diamond ring that Papa and Mama had given her for her birthday. She looked very pretty, though *she* didn't think so. She especially hates her nose – she calls it her 'humble stub'.

Maybe she isn't as pretty as Tatiana. Tatiana has auburn hair and grey eyes and she's very slim and graceful and never clumsy or loud – in fact the absolute opposite of me. I never seem to grow and I'm afraid my legs are distinctly short and fat. All the aunts and uncles and cousins came for the ball and there was lots of dancing and supper in between. I had lobster and two helpings of strawberry water ice. Everyone got hot so all the doors and windows were opened and you could see the most enormous orange moon outside almost falling into the sea. I can't wait to be sixteen.

September 9th, Tsarskoe Selo

Back home. I was happy to see everyone. Shura's mother, who works in the laundry here, has had another baby – her eleventh! Shura's the eldest – she's eighteen. She took me to see her new baby brother.

Lessons have started again, worse luck. We had Russian and history this morning with Sovanna and we gave her some flowers, because it was the first day of the school year. Sovanna is very clever. Her grandfather was a famous poet and she's always reciting long poems by him. I think you'd say she was very plain, except for when she smiles, which is not very often, and then she looks almost pretty. She believes that it's just as important for girls to be educated as boys and she's always talking about politics with Pyotr Vasilievich, who teaches us literature.

I asked Mama if I could comb her hair and choose her pearls before dinner – Tatiana usually does it, but I don't see why she always gets to do everything for Mama. Mama said yes. Her hair is auburn, like Tatiana's, and very, very long.

September 11th

After breakfast Marie and I helped the maids tidy our room. Jim Hercules – he's one of the Negroes who opens and closes the doors into our part of the palace – came back from his holiday in America and brought me a jar of something called guava jelly. He says it's very delicious with bread and butter. Jim and the other Negroes are over six feet tall and they have a special uniform – scarlet trousers, white turbans and shoes which curl up at the toes.

September 12th

Olga and Tatiana have gone to Kiev with Papa because Papa is going to unveil a statue of Grandpapa, who was Tsar Alexander III. It's very unfair – Olga and Tatiana always get to do things with Papa, like going to the theatre or the ballet, or to Kiev, just because they're older, while Marie and I are left behind. Lessons were boring. Mama has a headache.

Marie and I went bicycling. Alexis wanted to come with us, but of course we had to tell him he couldn't and then he had a tantrum. I do feel sorry for Alexis sometimes – there are so many things he can't do. Anyway, I had to go and get Nagorny and Derevenko. Nagorny and Derevenko used to be sailors but now their job is to watch Alexis all the time, to make sure he doesn't hurt himself. Derevenko brought his two sons to cheer Alexis up and they all took it in turns riding Alexis's donkey, Vanka, so it ended well! Vanka used to be a circus donkey and he knows all sorts of tricks, like sticking his nose in your pocket to find sugar lumps or india-rubber balls, which he especially loves for some strange reason.

September 15th

Olga and Tatiana have seen a murder! Last night they went to the theatre in Kiev with Papa and in the interval they heard a sort of bang, not very loud. They looked down from the box and saw Pyotr Stolypin – that's the Prime Minister – with blood on the front of his white shirt. He looked up at Papa and made the sign of the cross and then he sat down in his seat, very slowly. A man had just walked right up to him and shot him in the chest. People were holding the man and ladies were screaming. He's not actually dead yet, but he's very badly hurt. Papa is going to see him in hospital. Why does nothing exciting ever happen to me?

September 19th

Pyotr Stolypin died today. Mama says that Our Friend knew he would die and Sovanna says that Stolypin was the only man who could save Russia and it's a very sad day for us all. I asked Sovanna what she meant about saving Russia and she said that Russia needs to change and Stolypin understood that and he was trying to make reforms, like giving peasants their own land, and that made some people angry, which is why he was shot. I said that I thought he'd been shot by a revolutionary and she said, 'Well maybe he was and maybe he wasn't.' It's all very confusing. All I know is that revolutionaries are bad and I'm sure Papa will punish them.

September 21st

While we were walking in the park this afternoon, I heard Sovanna talking to Pyotr Vasilievich. She said that with Pyotr Stolypin gone she feared for the future. So I called out, 'What are you so afraid of?' and she turned round, looking rather annoyed, and said, 'You shouldn't be listening to grown-up conversation Anastasia Nicolaevna – why don't you go down to the lake with Alexis?' But I didn't. Pyotr Vasilievich kept shaking his head in a mournful way and then he said something like – I couldn't hear properly – 'If the Tsar doesn't listen... nothing less than revolution.' This made me think about the revolution in France, which we did in history, and how the King and Queen were sent to the guillotine. So later I asked Mama if there could ever be a revolution here in Russia. Her face went all blotchy, like it does when she's upset, and she said, 'Don't be ridiculous, Anastasia, you know how the Russian people worship their Tsar.'

October 9th

Sunday. We walked to church. Afterwards Aunt Olga came, like she does every Sunday, to take me and my sisters to St Petersburg. We went on the train and we talked non-stop all the way. Aunt Olga is very jolly and she says it's good for us to get out of Tsarskoe Selo and to see other children.

First we went to have lunch with Grandmama at the Anitchkov Palace, which is where she lives when she's in town. Grandmama has lovely sparkly black eyes, a bit like

Aunt Olga, but she's quite strict and she's always saying I must learn not to be so noisy and to stop rushing. She told us stories about Grandpapa, who was Tsar Alexander III, and how he was more than six feet tall – much taller than Papa – and so strong that he could crash through locked doors and bend iron pokers with his bare hands. Once he and Grandmama and Papa and the other children were on a train that crashed and he held up the roof with his shoulders so everyone could crawl out. Grandmama said, 'Grandpapa did sometimes have the manners of a bear, but I couldn't have wished for a better husband,' and she looked quite sorrowful.

After lunch we went to my aunt's house for tea and games and dancing. It was the greatest fun. In fact Sunday at my aunt's is my favourite day.

October 30th

I did my imitation of Count Fredericks, doing his stiff little bow and stroking his moustache, for Ania and Grandmama and some other people, and they all laughed. Then later Count Fredericks came up to me in the drawing room and said – 'Good evening, Your Imperial Highness. A little bird told me you've been making a study of me.' I didn't know what to say. It was very embarrassing, even though he looked quite twinkly.

I wish Count Fredericks wouldn't call me 'Imperial Highness'. I've asked him not to, but he goes on doing it.

November 18th

It snowed today, but not enough yet for tobogganing. The hairdresser came from St Petersburg to cut our hair. We walked to Ania's house for tea and saw Our Friend. He was sitting next to me and I couldn't help noticing that he was awfully stinky. Afterwards I asked Marie if *she'd* noticed and she said, 'What, you mean that old bear skin kind of smell?' So I said, 'Yes – an old bear skin that's been peed on!' And Marie said, 'And what about all those bits of dried-up cabbage in his beard?' By this time we were laughing so much we had to lie down. Then Olga came in and asked us what we were giggling about, but we wouldn't tell her because she'd have disapproved – she thinks Our Friend is practically a saint. I know we shouldn't laugh at him. He's probably just too holy to wash.

November 27th

This morning Dr Botkin said he was going to send a nurse to give me a massage for my back (they say it's weak). I don't want to have a massage. He also said I shouldn't climb trees. I intend to ignore him.

Usually I like Dr Botkin. He has a way of saying things very seriously, when you know he's not being serious at all and he behaves as if he's an old man, when in fact he's the same age as Papa. His wife died after Tatiana – that's his daughter – was born, so Tatiana and her brother Gleb live with their grandmother in Tsarskoe Selo.

November 30th

Walked to Znamenia for mass and then confession with Father Vasilev. In the evening Olga and Mama went to church again, but I refused. I can't understand why Olga loves church *so* much. She always gets a silly look on her face when she's there, as if she's just eaten a huge bowl of strawberry ice cream, or she's actually seeing God or something. I suppose she's just very religious. The nurse came to give me a massage and I hid under the bed.

December 3rd

I had my French lesson with Monsieur Gilliard. He's from Switzerland and he's mostly Alexis's tutor, but he also teaches us girls French. After lessons Olga, Tatiana and I went skating on the big lake. Alexis wasn't allowed, so he went in the donkey sledge with Nagorny and Derevenko. I crashed into Tatiana and she was furious because her new cape – it's lined with white rabbit – got torn. She told me I was a clumsy oaf and I said, 'Well, I'd rather be a clumsy oaf than a stuck-up madam.' She said she'd tell Mama, which is what she always does. She's a tell-tattle and she's always bossing us, even Olga. Alexis calls her 'the Governess', which she hates.

December 6th

Mama took us girls to St Petersburg to see the *Nutcracker* ballet at the Maryinsky theatre. Anna Pavlova, who's a very famous ballerina, was the little girl. It was wonderful. The Maryinsky is all blue and gold inside – it's like being in a jewel box. In the interval we had lemonade and lemon ice cream. There were masses of children there, who walked past us and stared. We got back to Tsarskoe Selo at midnight.

December 13th

Did Christmas cards all afternoon. Marie kept asking me what I was writing in mine and then putting exactly the same in hers, which is absolutely typical of her. So when she wasn't looking I grabbed the card she'd done for Mr Gibbes and put hundreds of kisses all over it and of course she cried and of course Tatiana said, 'You two really are a pair of babies.'

I'm also making Christmas presents – bookmarks for Papa and the uncles and pin cushions for Grandmama and the aunts. I'm copying a poem that Sovanna has found for me with a drawing around it, for Mama. I'm going to share other presents, to Count Fredericks and Ania and Orchie and Sovanna and Mr Gibbes and Monsieur Gilliard, with my sisters. We have a special signature – **ОТМЯ**. That's our initials. It saves time!

1912

January 1st

It's a new year! I must remember to write '1912'. For the first time I was allowed to stay up till midnight for the New Year Te Deum* in the palace chapel.

January 8th

This morning I had French with Monsieur Gilliard, then history with Sovanna. Sovanna talked about Tsar Alexander II, who was Papa's grandpapa and is her absolute hero because he freed the serfs. The serfs were peasants that people owned, like slaves. But even though Alexander II was such a good man he was still blown up by a revolutionary, which Papa says just goes to show what sort of people revolutionaries are. Papa can remember (he was thirteen) seeing his grandpapa lying on a couch in the

---

* Words marked with a star are explained in a glossary at the back of the book.

Winter Palace, with his legs torn off, bleeding to death.

January 11th

Sunday – so we went to Aunt Olga's in St Petersburg. There was a magic lantern show. In the evening, after we'd got ready for bed, Our Friend came in to say prayers with us in front of the icon. Sometimes when we pray together I really do feel that God is right there in the room. Sovanna gets very sarcastic about Our Friend – she calls him 'that filthy peasant' and says she doesn't know why Papa lets him spend so much time creeping about our rooms. I've told her that he's a starets but she just snorts and says that he certainly doesn't behave like one. I think she just doesn't like him because he's rather dirty and smelly. She doesn't understand how he helps us and especially how he helps Alexis.

January 14th

I'm in bed with a bad cold. Alexis has been sitting with me and showing me his collection of nails (for some reason he likes nails). I said, 'You don't have to sit here with me all day,' and he said, 'I know how it feels to have to stay in bed – I'd like to think I can cheer you up.' Then he gave me his best nail! I must admit that even though Alexis is often aggravating and extremely naughty, he can surprise you. Sometimes he seems much more grown-up than eight.

January 18th

Dr Botkin said I could go out again today. You always

know when Dr Botkin has been in the room because you can smell his perfume – it's called eau-de-cologne, from Paris, and it's an oranges and lemons kind of smell. So today Marie and I decided to follow his scent, like bloodhounds. We sniffed all the way from the nursery, down to Mama's little sitting room, into the drawing room, through the round hall, into the other side of the palace and to the drawing room that the ladies and gentlemen of Papa and Mama's suite use and then we gave a huge sniff and said, 'Found you Dr Botkin!' and he looked quite surprised. This afternoon Monsieur Gilliard, Nagorny and Derevenko helped us build a giant snow mountain for tobogganing, but it got dark before we could try it out.

February 20th

Had pancakes for luncheon for the last time because tomorrow is the first day of Lent.

February 24th

Marie and I helped the maids tidy our room. Mama's heart was bad, so she stayed in her room all day. Very good tobogganing down the snow mountain. Went for tea at Ania's. Her parents were there and also Our Friend. Ania does tend to suck up to people (like Marie, but worse). She kept saying, 'Oh, Olga Nicolaevna, you do play the piano so beautifully,' and, 'Oh, Tatiana Nicolaevna, you're looking so pretty.' I noticed she didn't say anything about me.

March 2nd

This morning it was my English lesson with Mr Gibbes. He only gave me three out of five marks for my dictation, even though it was nearly all right. I asked him if he'd give me five and he said no. So I went and got a huge bunch of flowers from the nursery and I gave them to him and said, 'Are you going to change the marks, Mr Gibbes?' He just shook his head. Then I went into the other schoolroom, where Pyotr Vasilievich was teaching Tatiana, and I said 'Pyotr Vasilievich, allow me to present you with these flowers,' and he took them! Mr Gibbes looked quite perplexed.

He never laughs when we tease him (not like Pyotr Vasilievich) and he hates it if we ask him questions about England and his family and whether he wants to get married. The only things he's ever told us are that he has ten brothers and sisters and he prefers Russia to England.

Olga says it's normal for Englishmen to be reserved. I asked her if I was reserved and she said, 'Most definitely not.' But I think Tatiana is, even though she's only one quarter English.

March 7th

Something odd happened this afternoon. I came into the nursery and saw Shura with Our Friend – she was standing up against the wall and he was stroking her hair. At least that's what it looked like. He turned round and saw me and said, 'Ah, Anastasia, I was just blessing our dear Shura,' and she ran out of the room without looking at me.

This evening, when Shura was helping me get ready for bed, I asked her what she'd been doing with Our Friend and she went bright red and said she didn't want to talk about it. I've just told Marie and she said that probably Our Friend was just putting his hand on Shura's head, not stroking her hair. Anyway, he often strokes our hair. But why was she upset? I shan't mention this to Sovanna.

March 19th

The snow has nearly all melted. Went for a bicycle ride with Marie and Tatiana. When we came back I left my bicycle by the steps and when I wasn't looking Alexis took it and went off, wobbling, towards the lake. Papa called out to him to stop, but he didn't take any notice and suddenly everyone started shouting and running. Nagorny caught him and carried him back and Papa looked really quite angry, which he hardly ever is. He said, 'You are never, never to do that, Alexis,' and gave him a kind of hug that was also a shake.

Alexis can be very naughty – he's often disobedient with Monsieur Gilliard. A few days ago, when he was supposed to be writing out French verbs, he kept jumping up and fiddling with his catapult. After Monsieur Gilliard had asked him for about the hundredth time to sit down, he said, 'One day I'll be tsar and no one will be able to tell me what to do.' Monsieur Gilliard replied, 'It's precisely because you're going to be tsar that your education is so important,' which I thought was a pretty good answer. The problem with Alexis is that nobody likes to tell him off.

March 27th

Papa has taken Mama to a spa in Germany, which Dr Botkin says will be good for her heart. It feels very strange without them. Orchie walked in the park with us and I asked her what Mama was like as a girl. She said that when she was very little everyone called her 'Sunny' because she was so merry. But after her own mama died of diphtheria, when Mama was six, and her sister died too and all Mama's toys were burned to stop the infection, she became quite quiet and serious. Then I asked if Mama had been good at her lessons and Orchie said, 'Well, she worked a good deal harder than you do, Anastasia Nicolaevna.' Which wouldn't be difficult.

April 3rd

Ania brought Our Friend to have tea with us today. Later, when we were ready for bed, he came and sat in Olga and Tatiana's room and talked to us. Then we prayed together. When Sovanna came to say goodnight she said, 'I hope that man hasn't been in here again,' and Olga said he hadn't! Olga hates lying, but she says that as Sovanna just doesn't understand about Our Friend it's for the best.

April 4th

Alexis and I got into trouble for throwing bread pellets at luncheon and Tatiana called us 'tiresome children', as if she wasn't only fifteen herself. One of our pellets hit Mr Gibbes on the chest and he made a great fuss and said that it had made a mark on his jacket and he had to go and change. Monsieur Gilliard said, 'It's only a bit of bread,' which just made him crosser. Mr Gibbes is very particular – he's always checking his cuffs for specks of dirt.

April 10th

Papa and Mama are home! Mama says she feels her heart is definitely better, but she missed us all terribly. I told her what I'd been talking about with Orchie and she said, 'Well, I think it's because I lost my own mama that I can hardly bear to be away from you precious girlies and baby for a minute.' We're getting ready to go to Livadia for Easter.

April 17th, Livadia

It rained all day so we couldn't go out. Painted Easter eggs.

April 21st

I'm very sad Easter is over. It's the most holy festival of the year. We went to the midnight service, which is my favourite service of all. Everyone walks in a procession around the church, carrying candles and then we stop in front of the altar and the priest says, 'Christ is risen!' and we reply, 'Yes indeed. He is risen,' and everyone gives each other three kisses.

On Easter Day masses of people came to the palace and Papa and Mama kissed them all (three times) and we helped hand out eggs – the most important people get gold and enamel eggs while everyone else gets china ones. Then we ate and ate. I had masses of kulich* and paskha*. Mama had her egg from Papa, made by Mr Faberge. This one has a clock on it and when the o'clock strikes a gold cockerel comes out of the top of the egg and flaps its wings! Later lots of children from the nearby villages came and we girls gave them all Easter cakes.

April 30th

The Emir of Bokhara came to see Papa yesterday. He has an incredibly long black beard and he wears a kind of robe all covered in gold and silver and diamonds. He brought two ministers who have beards that are dyed bright red. Even though the Emir can speak Russian perfectly he always has an interpreter and he always brings wonderful presents. He gave Mama a gold necklace which looks like a snake and has rubies all over it.

May 11th

The wisteria and the roses are coming out everywhere and the smell is delicious. Yesterday it was the White Flower Festival – it raises money for the people who have tuberculosis in the sanatoriums. We all dressed up in white dresses with big hats (Alexis wore his sailor suit) and we carried long sticks covered in white margaritas. Then we stood outside the bazaar with money boxes around our necks and looked encouragingly at people as they came in. Nearly everyone bought some margaritas. Alexis made the most money, but that's just because he's the Tsarevich and everyone wants to talk to him.

May 16th, Tsarskoe Selo

Aunt Ella has come to stay. Aunt Ella is Mama's older sister and I think she's the most beautiful person I know, after Mama and Tatiana. Her husband, Uncle Serge, was blown up in his carriage by a revolutionary. When Aunt Ella heard the explosion she ran out into the street and picked up the bits of Uncle Serge that were left – just his head, and an arm and a foot – and put them on a stretcher, which was jolly brave of her I think.

I didn't actually like Uncle Serge very much. He was awfully thin and bony and he wore corsets, which creaked when he embraced you, and he hardly ever spoke to Aunt Ella. Now Aunt Ella is an abbess. She's built her own abbey in Moscow and she always wears her white abbess dress and a veil. She could be a saint. I showed her the photographs that I took at Livadia.

June 1st, Peterhof

Got my pocket money. We're at Alexandria, our dacha at Peterhof. It's by the sea, on the Gulf of Finland, and it's all made of wood, much smaller than the Alexander Palace and very cosy. After lessons we went canoeing with Papa.

There's a summer house here and on one of its windows you can see 'Nicky and Alix June 8 1884'. That's Papa and Mama! It was when they first met, when Mama came to Russia for Aunt Ella's wedding to Uncle Serge.

Mama was only twelve, but Papa says he noticed her at once because she was so pretty. After the wedding, when she came to stay at Peterhof, he showed her around the park and they scratched their names on the window. He also gave her a brooch, but she gave it back to him because she wasn't sure she should accept a present from a boy. I always go and look at the window when I'm here.

June 12th, on our yacht

We've been on the *Standart* – our yacht – for three days. Mama has had to stay at Peterhof because of her heart. Tatiana wanted to stay as well – she always wants to be the one to look after Mama – but Mama wouldn't let her. We write to her every day. Living on a ship is the greatest fun. You can almost forget it's a ship because it's so enormous and inside the rooms look just like the Alexander Palace. Every day we take a little boat and go ashore with Papa for a swim. Sometimes we walk on the beach and look for shells and pebbles and interesting objects.

Last night, after tea, the balalaika orchestra played and we took photographs of each other making faces. The sailors are so friendly and jolly.

June 14th

Yesterday Uncle Willy came and moored his yacht beside ours. Uncle Willy is the Kaiser of Germany and he's also Mama's cousin, though I don't think she likes him very much. He was in love with Aunt Ella when they were young, but she refused him, which I can quite understand, but then I don't understand why she preferred to marry Uncle Serge.

Uncle Willy was born with a withered arm, but it's hidden under his jacket, so you can hardly see it. He struts about, all puffed up like a peacock, and he talks non-stop – usually boasting. His yacht isn't as big as ours, and it's not as beautiful either and when he came on board this morning he said, 'Well, I must say I'd be very happy if someone wanted to give me the *Standart* as a present.' So I said, 'Perhaps you should start saving up Uncle Willy.' Papa frowned at me, but Uncle Willy sort of laughed. Later he said, 'Haven't any of these handsome fellows' – he meant the officers – 'caught your eye, young lady?' He's always saying stupid things like that.

June 21st, Tsarskoe Selo

They're making hay in the park – Marie, Alexis and I went and rolled around in it and buried each other. It's the White Nights at the moment, which means it hardly gets dark at all and we're allowed to stay up till eleven.

June 30th

Sovanna has been dismissed. I'm not sure why, but I think it's because of the bad things she's been saying about Our Friend. Tatiana says Sovanna told Mama that she didn't think he should come and pray with us when we were in our nightgowns. What *did* she mean? She didn't even come to say goodbye.

July 1st

Aunt Olga came for lunch. I told her about Sovanna leaving and how stupid she'd been about Our Friend and Aunt Olga said that she thought that even though Sovanna had some rather strange opinions, perhaps she wasn't altogether wrong about Our Friend. But I know Aunt Olga doesn't much like him either – she always leaves the room if he comes to see us while she's here.

July 4th

Papa has gone to meet the French President. I miss him. Went riding with Olga and Marie in the afternoon.

July 7th

Papa came home last night. He brought us presents from the French President. I've got a doll, from Paris. She looks a bit like Marie. She's got the same yellowy-brown hair and round blue eyes – Marie's eyes are so big we call them her 'saucers'.

The doll has a whole trunk of clothes – lace petticoats and underthings and silk dresses and hats. It's called a trousseau. There's a dressing table with tiny hairbrushes and even a powder puff. Actually I don't terribly like dolls, and besides I'm too old for them. Alexis got a model factory, with tiny doll workers, who start working when you press a button.

August 20th, on the train

We're on our way to Poland, to our hunting lodges at Bieloveji and Spala. Before dinner, when we were in the dining car having zakouski*, Alexis got hold of a glass of champagne and drank it all! Then he became very silly and made the ladies laugh.

August 28th, Bieloveji

Papa went hunting. When he came back we went for a long ride through the woods. Alexis rowed on the lake. He slipped when he was getting out of the boat and hurt his leg, at the top.

September 9th

Alexis has been in bed and Derevenko has been massaging his leg every day and now it's not nearly so swollen. We're going to Spala next week.

September 23rd, Spala

We've arrived at our lodge. It's a wooden house, right in the middle of the woods, and it's always dark – you have to keep the electric lights on even in the day time. Lots of guests have come to go hunting with Papa.

September 27th

Alexis is very ill. Yesterday, Mama and Ania took him for a drive and they hadn't gone very far when he got a very bad pain in his leg, so they came home at once. Now he's in bed and he's screaming his head off and his left leg is all

45

bent up. Dr Botkin says he has a haemorrhage inside and it's probably from when he fell in the boat.

Mama sits with him most of the time, but she won't let us see him. I think she's awfully worried – she was crying when she came out of his room this evening.

September 30th

I think Alexis is worse. He screams horribly – the servants have put cotton wool in their ears so they can't hear him. Professor Fedorov, who's a very important doctor, is coming tomorrow from Moscow. Papa went hunting. We had lessons as usual. Monsieur Gilliard is rehearsing a French play with Marie and me. It's called *Bourgeois Gentilhomme* and we have to speak in French! It's supposed to be a distraction.

October 6th

I stood outside Alexis's door and I could hear him moaning and crying 'Lord have mercy on us.' The doctors can't stop the bleeding. I'm terribly afraid he might die. If he dies who would be the next Tsar?

Alexis has a disease called haemophilia which means his blood doesn't clot, and it's not something that gets better. No one talks about it. The guests aren't supposed to know there's anything the matter, but they must be able to hear him screaming. Mama never leaves him except to go to dinner and then she hardly eats anything. I've been praying as hard as I can. Last night Marie and I performed *Bourgeois Gentilhomme* in the dining room for Mama and

Papa, the suite and the guests. Everyone clapped a lot and Monseiur Gilliard only had to prompt me twice, so I think it was alright.

October 8th

There's no church here, so instead, when we arrived, a big green tent, with an altar in it, was put up in the forest. Now Father Vasilev has started saying prayers there for Alexis twice a day. All the servants and the Cossacks and masses of Polish peasants come and pray with us. Mama says people are praying all over Russia. Marie and I played tennis with Papa.

October 9th

At luncheon Papa was handed a note, from Mama, and he left the room immediately. He's been in Alexis's room ever since and Father Vasilev is in there too. No one tells us anything. Please don't let Alexis die.

October 11th

He isn't going to die! Mama says it's a miracle. She sent a telegram to Our Friend, asking him to pray for Alexis, and he sent one back, which she showed us. It said – 'The Little One will not die. Do not allow the doctors to bother him too much.' And the next day the bleeding stopped!

This morning we had communion, with the servants and the Cossacks, to thank God, and then Father Vasilev took the cup to Alexis. I asked Papa what would have happened if Alexis had died and there wasn't an heir any more and he said that God was watching over Alexis and I mustn't ever think about him dying. So then I said, 'But don't you sometimes wish Mama had had lots of boys, like Aunt Xenia, instead of all us girls?' And he pinched my cheek and said, 'What would I do without my girls, and especially my Anastasia and her funny ways?' I do love Papa.

October 29th

Alexis is still in bed. He's very thin, but he's better. We take it in turns to try and amuse him. Today Mr Gibbes and I helped him with his model village and then I did my imitation of Fat Orlov trying to get onto his horse, which does look ridiculous because he can't actually get on his horse any more – he's too fat. Mama's hair has gone quite grey.

November 17th, Tsarskoe Selo

I'm glad to be home at last. It was Count Fredericks's birthday today. He's 75. We – that's 'OTMA' – gave him six silk handkerchiefs that we'd embroidered with his initials.

November 25th

I've been in bed with influenza for three days, but my temperature is normal today. Tatiana and Marie have also been ill. Yesterday Mama came to sit with me and I asked her to tell me the story of how she married Papa (my favourite story!). She said that she first fell in love with him when she was seventeen and came to Russia to stay with Aunt Ella. It was the season in St Petersburg and she and Papa went to lots of balls and suppers and he was such a good dancer that he made her feel as if *she* could dance (Mama doesn't really like dancing). They went for midnight troika* rides along the banks of the Neva and it was very romantic. He asked her to marry him but she said she couldn't because of her religion. She was Protestant and she didn't think she could be Russian Orthodox. But she didn't forget Papa and his kind blue eyes.

Then, when she was 22, she went to Coburg for Uncle Ernst's wedding (Ernst is her brother) and Papa was there, with lots of other Royalties like Great Granny (she was Queen Victoria), and she knew she still loved him. She had a long talk with Aunt Ella who told her how she hadn't minded converting a bit and how she'd come to love the Russian Orthodox Church. So when Papa came to see her and asked her again, she said yes.

The first thing they had to do was to tell Great Granny, which made them feel quite nervous because they knew Great Granny didn't like Russia at all. They found her finishing her breakfast and she was very nice to them. She said, 'It's a very great position for you, Alicky. Don't get proud!' and later she told Mama that Papa had beautiful manners.

Mama went home to Darmstadt for a while, but then she came to Russia. She married Papa just a few weeks after Papa's father died, which Mama said felt quite strange and not very joyful, because everyone was in mourning and

Motherdear (that's what she calls Grandmama) couldn't stop crying. But she and Papa were so happy they didn't mind.

December 22nd

Today's my name day – that means the day on which the saint you're named after is celebrated. It also means presents! Papa and Mama gave me a silver bracelet, some notebooks and a tablecloth with the story of *The Snow Queen* embroidered round the edge. Our Friend sent me a telegram. It said, 'My little Anastasia! Greetings on your name day! May the Lord help you to carry your cross with wisdom and joy!' And there was a special Te Deum in Znamenia. My name day is very close to Christmas, but actually it's nicer than Christmas.

1913

January 3rd, Tsarskoe Selo

Went to mass with Papa and Aunt Olga. Mama had a pain in her face and her head, so she stayed in her room. In the afternoon Papa, Marie and I tobogganed down the bank above the narrow pond. It was incredibly steep and icy and we simply whizzed. Alexis's leg is still in a brace and he's not allowed to go out yet. Our Friend came to see us in the evening. He talked to Papa and Mama and then we prayed together. Afterwards we all felt very peaceful.

January 19th

In our English lesson with Mr Gibbes this morning Alexis suddenly put down his pen and said, 'I must have a sweet.' I think Mr Gibbes doesn't dare to say no to him at the moment, so Derevenko was sent off and he came back with a chocolate sitting all by itself on a glass dish, which he put in front of Alexis, who ate it very slowly. My sisters and I would never be allowed to do that.

February 7th

This year it's the anniversary of our family, the Romanovs, ruling Russia for 300 years. There are going to be great celebrations and we're going to St Petersburg tomorrow.

February 11th, Winter Palace

It's funny staying here. It's so big and gloomy and there's no park – it doesn't feel like home at all. Yesterday there was a Te Deum in the cathedral. We drove there in carriages, from the palace. I was in a carriage with Aunt Olga and my sisters. You couldn't believe how Nevsky Prospect was jammed with people and carriages – it took ages to go just a tiny way. There were red, white and blue streamers and banners everywhere and lots of pictures of all the tsars of Russia. When we arrived at the cathedral there was the most enormous crowd outside and they all knelt down. During the service two doves flew down from the dome and sort of fluttered over Papa's and Alexis's heads – Papa thinks the doves were sent by God, as a sign of his blessing and I think he's right. In the evening we went onto the balcony of the palace to watch the *son et lumière*.

February 14th

Yesterday there was a big reception here, in the throne

room, and we were allowed to attend. We wore white dresses with silver thread and the Order of St Catherine, which is a scarlet ribbon with diamonds all over it – almost as good as proper jewels. We had to stand for hours and hours and be presented to people and it was really very boring. I dared Alexis to pinch Fat Orlov on the bottom with a lobster claw and he did! But Papa saw him and was furious and he was taken away by Monsieur Gilliard. Later I owned up – that it was my idea.

Mama has had one of her headaches – she says it's all these balls and receptions. Tonight there's a special opera at the Marinksy called *A Life for the Tsar*, and Mama doesn't want to go. I heard Grandmama saying to her, 'My dear Alix, you really must go. You have to understand that people expect to *see* you,' and Mama looked as if she might cry. Grandmama is sometimes a bit impatient with Mama. She doesn't understand how Mama suffers.

February 23rd, Tsarskoe Selo
I'm very glad to be home. We have a new governess now, Mademoiselle Schneider. She's not nearly as strict as Sovanna, but her lessons aren't as interesting and she never recites poetry for us. I wish Sovanna hadn't left.

March 30th
I'm going to breed worms. I've collected six worms and put them in a box, full of earth, with glass sides, in the nursery. It's called a wormery. So far there are still only six, but I think they need time to settle in. Of course I can't be

sure if they're male or female, but I'm going to observe them and take notes.

Tatiana says the wormery stinks, which is nonsense as everyone knows worms don't smell, and that I can't keep it in the nursery. I'm absolutely sick of being bossed about by Tatiana – she's not even the eldest, but she behaves as if she is and Olga lets her. I told Olga what an absolute swine Tatiana was being and she said, 'Oh, Anastasia, she's probably right – it's not worth arguing with Tatiana.' Olga just doesn't seem to care – she's too busy reading or praying. She'll probably grow up to be an abbess like Aunt Ella.

April 3rd

Tatiana kept complaining about the wormery and now Orchie has made me get rid it. Alexis is outside doing military manoeuvres in his Cossack uniform. We're going to Livadia tomorrow.

April 11th, Livadia

Easter. Papa gave Mama a special egg. It has portraits of all the tsars and empresses there have ever been and inside there's a tiny globe with maps of the Russian Empire.

April 14th

Went to Ai-Todor for the day. Our cousins, Maria and Dmitri, were there. Their father is Uncle Pavel – he's Papa's uncle, which makes him our great uncle. Their mother died when they were very young and then Uncle Pavel married someone without Papa's permission so he went and lived abroad, and Maria and Dmitri were looked after by Aunt Ella and Uncle Serge because they didn't have any children of their own.

Maria is married to a Swedish prince, but she says she doesn't like living in Sweden. She can be rather spiteful and mean about people behind their backs. Dmitri's very nice and funny, though he does fuss about his clothes all the time. Orchie says a man should have better things to think about than his appearance.

May 11th, on a steamboat

We're making a pilgrimage – it's part of the celebrations. Right now we're steaming along the Volga and it's exactly the same journey that the very first tsar, Michael Romanov, made when he was sixteen, from the place that he was born, to Moscow, where he was crowned.

I do like being on the steamboat – you can easily see the houses along the banks and people run out and bow to us and cheer. Sometimes peasants wade into the river, right up to their waists, in order to get closer to the boat. Mama says that it just shows how the peasants really love Papa.

Yesterday evening, while we were sitting on deck, Alexis asked Papa, 'If I'm tsar will everyone in Russia have to obey me?' Papa gave a kind of laugh and said, 'It's not *if*, but *when*, Alexis, and you must understand that as tsar you'll be responsible for many millions of people – it's a very sacred duty.' Alexis just said, 'Yes, but they'll still have to obey me, won't they?' Honestly!

May 14th

Poor Mr Gibbes – I think he's fed up with us. During our English lesson yesterday Alexis kept fooling around with some scissors and Mr Gibbes kept asking him to put them down – they're dangerous for him – but Alexis just ignored him and reached up and cut off a big piece of his hair. Then I grabbed the scissors and said, 'Mr Gibbes, I think you need a little haircut' (Mr Gibbes's hair is always very neat and tidy). And Marie and I started chasing him around the cabin with the scissors until he exclaimed, 'This is really too much!' and stormed out. He almost looked as though he might cry. Then we all felt quite guilty and had to apologise. Later Alexis and I sat on deck and played our balalaikas and people waved and clapped as we went past.

June 8th, Moscow

Yesterday Papa rode into the city all by himself, with the Cossacks behind him. Mama and Alexis followed in a motor with no roof and we girls were in another motor. In Red Square Papa got off his horse and walked for the last bit, into the Kremlin. Alexis was meant to walk with him, but his leg still isn't better, so he was carried by one of the Cossacks. You could see people pointing and murmuring as he went past. Papa and Mama have been awfully worried about people saying that there was something wrong with Alexis, but they want to see him because he's the heir, so it would have been worse if he hadn't been there at all.

On the way back from the Kremlin Alexis's motor got stuck in a great crowd of people, who recognised him and started shouting, 'The Heir! The Heir!' and reaching out to try and touch him. Monsieur Gilliard had to put out his arms, like a shield, until the police arrived and cleared everyone away. Alexis looked quite pale and shaky when he arrived home. The celebrations are over now.

September 12th, Livadia

Haven't written this for the whole time we've been at Livadia and tomorrow we go back to Tsarskoe Selo! I never much feel like writing my diary here – it's too much like work. Anyway, mostly we've just been loafing around, riding, playing tennis, no lessons. Bliss. There was a charity bazaar in Yalta to raise money for the sanatoriums, so we all had to make things. I did a lot of watercolours and embroidered cushion covers, which I couldn't imagine anyone would want to buy, but in fact Marie and I sold everything on our stall and we made over 100 roubles.

Otherwise divorce and marriage have been the topics of conversation. My cousin Maria wants to get divorced from her husband, the Swedish prince. She's come back to Russia because she's so unhappy. At least that's what Grandmama says. But the great news is that Irina, my other cousin, has become engaged to Felix Yusupov! I think Felix is extremely handsome, but Mama told Aunt Xenia that she would never let a daughter of *hers* marry him. I don't know why. I asked Olga and she didn't know either, but she thinks that Felix has a bad character.

A few days ago Aunt Xenia, Uncle Sandro, Irina and Felix came for tea. Felix beat Papa at tennis (Papa says he's the best player in the whole of Russia) and Irina showed us the jewels that Felix had given her – a pink diamond ring, a pink diamond and pearl necklace and a sapphire spray brooch. She says that his parents have given her masses more.

October 22nd, Tsarskoe Selo

Aunt Ella has come to stay. Yesterday, while I was in my room, I heard her and Aunt Olga down on the terrace. They were talking about Our Friend. Aunt Ella said, 'I hear there are women seen leaving his apartment at all hours.' And Aunt Olga replied, 'Yes, and the whole of St Petersburg is saying the most dreadful things about him and Alix.' Aunt Ella gave a great sigh and said, 'Oh why can't Nicky and Alix see him for what he *is?* Then Aunt Olga sort of whispered, 'Do you know he actually started stroking my arm the last time I saw him here?' 'What *do* they mean?' I asked Orchie and she looked very cross and said, 'Little pitchers have big ears,' which doesn't make sense either. So then I asked Olga and she got very red in the face and said that our aunts shouldn't say bad things about a Man of God. I agree with her.

November 11th

Olga and Tatiana had to go to Krasnoe Selo to review their

regiments. They wear proper uniforms, but with skirts not trousers. I can't wait to be colonel-in-chief of my own regiment. It's very frustrating always being last to do everything.

December 24th

Papa took us girls (Alexis isn't well, so he stayed behind with Mama) to St Petersburg, to see Grandmama. We went to a Te Deum in the cathedral with Aunt Xenia and the cousins and then we went back to the Anitchkov Palace for the Christmas tree and a big dinner. We've also got our own trees at Tsarskoe Selo, in the big sitting room and the nursery – they're decorated with glass balls that Mama had when she was a girl, and millions of candles.

1914

January 12th

It's Tatiana's name day today – she got a brooch and some ivory combs. I had literature this morning with Pyotr Vasilievich. We're reading a book by Turgenev. Pyotr Vasilievich says it's only by reading the great Russian writers that you truly come to understand the Russian soul. The trouble is I really don't enjoy reading much, unlike Olga, who's an absolute bookworm. Pyotr Vasilievich said, 'If you'd only apply yourself, Anastasia Nicolaevna, you'd have the makings of a good student.' So I said, 'But Pyotr Vasilievich, there are so many other things to apply oneself to,' and he just rolled his eyes.

I do like Pyotr Vasilievich. He doesn't mind when we tease him. He's quite old now and his wife died of cholera a long time ago. He has one son, who he worries about because he's become a socialist. Tonight we're going to St

Petersburg with Papa, to see Nijinsky – he's very famous – dancing at the Marinsky.

January 20th

Went to mass this morning at Znamenia and then confession. Aunt Olga came for tea. She told Mama that Nijinksy – he's the one we saw – has just been expelled from the Imperial Ballet because he offended Grandmama by wearing a costume that 'left absolutely nothing to the imagination'. I asked Aunt Olga what she meant. And she said, 'Oh, just rather tight.' Mama made a face and said, *'Pas devant les enfants,'* which is stupid because I understand French perfectly well, and in fact I also understand what Aunt Olga meant about Nijinksy's costume. We all did a puzzle after dinner while Papa read to us.

February 3rd

Grandmama is giving a ball tomorrow at the Anitchkov Palace for us – that's her granddaughters. I'm very excited. It will be my first ball, even though I'm not 'out' yet, of course. Olga and Tatiana are going to have their hair put up and they're also allowed to wear their diamonds.

February 5th

I think the ball might have been my best evening ever. The Anitchkov was all lit up by chandeliers and everything sparkled and smelled delicious, from all the orchids and lilies that Grandmama had ordered from the Crimea. We stood with Grandmama at the top of the main stairs to greet people. I wore a white dress with blue embroidery and blue satin shoes and I think I looked passable. We sat at round tables for dinner and I had lobster and sturgeon and a little bit of caviar, which I didn't like much, and pistachio ice cream. I had one glass of champagne as well, which made me rather giddy. I prefer mors* really. I danced the mazurka with my cousin Dmitri. I think he must be a very good dancer because he whirls and twirls you till you hardly know if you're upside down or the right way up. I also danced with Uncle Sandro and Papa.

Everyone said Tatiana was the most beautiful girl in the room. Mama left at midnight because she wasn't feeling well, but we stayed until 4.30! Then we took the train back to Tsarskoe Selo and had lots of tea and pirozhki*. Papa wanted to sleep, but we wouldn't stop talking. I didn't get up until one o'clock today.

February 23rd

Yesterday we all went to town for Felix and Irina's wedding. Felix got stuck in the elevator coming up to the chapel in the Anitchkov Palace and we had to rescue him by pulling on the cable! Irina came in on Papa's arm. She wore a satin dress embroidered with silver and a veil that once belonged to Marie Antoinette, who was the French Queen who got guillotined, and she looked very beautiful. During the ceremony you could see her shaking and halfway through she dropped her handkerchief, so I darted forward and picked it up for her. I don't understand why Mama and

Grandmama don't approve of Felix – I know Irina loves him.

After the ceremony there was a reception in the Winter Garden, with champagne and blinis and roe cutlets and baked apple pudding, all on gold plates. It went on for hours. At the end the gentlemen got a blue satin bag full of almonds and the ladies got a blue and white fan that said 'Anitchkov 1914' on it. We came back to Tsarskoe Selo in the evening.

March 9th

Tatiana has typhoid. She got ill after she went to St Petersburg with Mama. Now she's in bed and Dr Botkin and Mama are with her all the time. A specialist, from Moscow, is coming to see her. Olga biffed me in the schoolroom this morning because I was picking my nose.

March 21st

Tatiana is better, but she's very thin and weak. Luckily we're going to Livadia soon, so she can convalesce. After tea, I played the balalaika – I'm improving! – while Marie played the piano.

April 30th, Livadia

Papa and Mama have been talking to Olga about husbands. She's eighteen now, so she can get married. Some people have been saying she should marry Edward, who's the Prince of Wales in England. He's exactly the same age as Olga and we met him when we went to

England, but Olga says she didn't like him much. Now the Crown Prince of Rumania wants to marry her and Papa and Mama think that it's a good match.

Olga just says that she hates the idea of getting married and she wouldn't mind being a spinster and anyway she could never bear to leave Russia and live in another country. I agree with her – I'd like to get married and have lots of children, but I could only marry a Russian. I'd have to love him too, of course.

June 4th, on the Standart

We've sailed from Yalta to Constanza, which is in Rumania, so Olga can get to know her Crown Prince! Yesterday we met Prince Carol and his parents and the rest of his family. We had to go to the cathedral, then watch ships doing manoeuvres, then eat luncheon, then watch soldiers parading, then attend a huge banquet, then watch fireworks. At the (extremely dull) banquet Olga was put next to Prince Carol – I kept trying to catch her eye to wink at her.

It's a great relief to be back on the *Standart*, with just us. Olga says she feels humiliated being looked over like that and besides Prince Carol is the last person on earth she'd want to marry. He was very short and his eyes were a bit squinty and he hardly spoke to Olga, even when he was sitting next to her – he just stared at her all the time. When we were sitting on deck this evening Olga cried and said she couldn't bear it if Papa and Mama forced her to marry. Papa said, 'Of course no one's going to force you.' Then

Mama said that when she was a girl everyone, and especially Great Granny, hoped that she'd marry Prince Eddy of England (he was Great Granny's grandson), but when she met him she knew she couldn't possibly love him because he didn't take anything seriously and he had no chin at all, so she refused him. She also said that marrying Papa, the man she loved, was the greatest blessing of her life and she would never make any of us marry against our wishes.

Olga is very relieved. Actually I think Olga likes one of the officers on the *Standart* – she's always talking to him and giggling a lot, which is quite unlike her as she's usually a serious sort of person.

June 10th, Peterhof

We're here for just a few days, before our cruise. Ania came for dinner yesterday and afterwards Our Friend came and drank tea with us. Sometimes I can't help thinking about what my aunts said about him. I know we need him because he's the only person who can help Alexis and he's a great comfort to Mama, but I'm glad he's stopped coming into our room when we're getting ready for bed.

June 22nd, on the Standart

We're sailing in the Gulf of Finland. It's boiling hot. Luckily there's always a breeze on the boat and we go ashore and swim every day. When we were getting on board, two days ago, Alexis tried to jump onto the ladder, but slipped and caught his foot in a rung. Now his ankle is hurting him terribly.

June 28th

A telegram arrived for Papa today. It said that Archduke Franz Ferdinand has been shot in Sarajevo – that's the capital of Bosnia. He was shot by a Serbian man. Papa says there may be consequences – I'm not sure what that means, but the Archduke was the son of the Emperor of Austria, so the Austrians are bound to be angry.

Olga's officer thinks there could even be a war. He says Russia will have to help Serbia and Germany, who's Austria's ally, is not to be trusted. But Germany is ruled by Uncle Willy and he's Mama's cousin and our friend, so surely Uncle Willy wouldn't want to fight us? The balalaika orchestra played in the evening and we all sat on deck and absolutely sweltered, even though it was nine o'clock.

June 29th

Another telegram! Somebody has tried to kill Our Friend. He was in his village and a woman stabbed him in the stomach and now he may die. Mama has been crying and praying for him all day. Alexis's ankle is still swollen and he can't walk. There was dancing after dinner. Olga waltzed with her officer twice.

July 19th, Peterhof

It just seems to get hotter and hotter. We all, except Alexis, went canoeing with Papa. It's quite hard work trying to amuse Alexis. Monsieur Gilliard and Mr Gibbes read to him and helped him with his model ship. They quite often argue about whose turn it is to sit with Alexis – I think they both want to be his favourite. I did a puzzle with him this afternoon. Mostly he's very patient, but I suppose he's had to get used to being ill. I know I wouldn't be at all patient if I had to spend so much time in bed.

Some government ministers are coming tomorrow to have a meeting with Papa. Everyone is worried that there might be a war, but Papa says he can't believe Germany will let it come to that. They say Our Friend is going to get better.

July 21st

The President of France has come to visit Papa. There was a big banquet for him here last night, but Marie and I weren't allowed to go. I expect it was jolly dull, with all those courses and speeches and toasts. I helped Mama put on her diamonds and tiara. She said she had a headache and wished she could have a cosy dinner with us. There's nothing but talk of war.

August 1st

This evening we went to church and prayed as hard as we could for peace. Afterwards we were just sitting down for dinner when Papa was called to the telephone. We sat and waited and nobody spoke and I knew something bad had happened. Then Papa came back into the room. He looked at us all and then he said, very quietly, 'Germany has declared war on Russia.' Mama burst into tears and so did my sisters and I (Alexis just went red). Papa didn't eat dinner. Now he's in his study with his ministers and the ambassadors from England and France. Mama says it's all Uncle Willy's fault.

August 3rd, Winter Palace

We took the boat to St Petersburg, because Papa has to announce that we're at war. Poor Alexis had to stay at Peterhof. Thousands of people came to the palace for the service and Papa stood in front of the Vladimir Mother of God icon, which is one of our most beautiful and holy icons, and asked for its blessing. Then he said, 'I solemnly swear that I will never make peace so long as a single enemy remains on Russian soil.' It was very dramatic. Then Papa and Mama went out onto the balcony and there was the most tremendous cheering.

I peeped round the side of the door and I couldn't believe how many people were jammed into Palace Square, all kneeling down and singing the anthem. Everyone says we will easily beat the Germans and it'll all be over by Christmas.

August 18th, Moscow

Now we're in Moscow for a special ceremony, in the

Kremlin, to ask for God's blessing for the war. Papa and Mama are upset because Alexis's leg is hurting him a lot and he's desperate to be at the ceremony tomorrow.

August 19th

Alexis couldn't walk this morning, so he was carried into the Kremlin by a Cossack. At least he wasn't left behind. Aunt Ella came with us. In the cathedral we kissed the holy relics and then we walked behind Papa and Mama and knelt to pray in front of the tombs of the patriarchs. There were candles everywhere and great clouds of incense and it was very solemn and beautiful.

August 24th, Tsarskoe Selo

Home! Everything seems back to normal – I keep forgetting that we're at war. It's still very hot. We swam in the big lake, around the children's island, and it was as warm as a bath. Count Fredericks is getting very forgetful, because he's so old I suppose. He came up to Papa, when Papa was sitting in his study, and asked him if the Tsar had asked him to dinner. Papa said, 'My dear fellow, I *am* the Tsar!' St Petersburg is going to be called Petrograd from now on because 'Petersburg' sounds too German.

September 6th

Papa has gone to see the troops. In fact everything is different now, but not in a bad way – except for Papa having to be away so much. Mama, Ania, Olga and Tatiana go off every morning to the hospital that's been made in the Catherine Palace – we call it the 'big hospital'. They're training to be nurses and they wear nurses' uniforms. Marie and I are too young to be proper nurses. Typical. But there's another hospital here, in the Feodorovsky village, called after us – 'The Hospital of the Grand Duchesses Marie and Anastasia'. We're going to visit wounded soldiers there and help. It feels quite grown-up to have one's own hospital. We went with Mama to Znamenia to light a candle for Papa.

September 8th

Lessons have started again. Worse luck. Olga and Tatiana don't have them any more, because they're older and they're busy in the hospital. It's a great bore always being the youngest – well apart from Alexis that is. When Monsieur Gilliard made me conjugate *vouloir* for the third time I tried to strangle him (only pretend).

October 11th

Marie and I worked in the stores, where the troops can come and get all sorts of things that have been donated by rich people. We handed out food and blankets and clothes and the soldiers were jolly pleased and grateful, even though some of the clothes were rather dirty. It's a bit like playing shops. Aunt Olga was there too and we had a very merry time and didn't get home until eight o'clock.

October 23rd

I went to the station with Mama and Marie to meet our

hospital train. It was full of wounded men. Some of them had horrible injuries and groaned terribly. I think one man had lost his eyes – he just had a bloody bandage over them – and another had no legs and they were all filthy. But they smiled at us and said how glad they were to be coming to our hospital.

Later Marie and I went to see them there. The officers – there are four of them – have their own little rooms upstairs, and the ordinary soldiers are altogether downstairs. We walked around giving them cups of tea and asking them if they needed anything.

November 3rd

There's a soldier in our hospital who can't read or write, so I've offered to help him. He got a head wound in his very first battle, which is pretty bad luck. His name is Ivan Petrovich and he's just nineteen and comes from the Crimea, from a village I actually know because you drive through it on the way to Ai-Todor. When I told him that and also that the Crimea is one of my very favourite places, he looked quite delighted. He described his house – just three rooms that he shares with his parents, three brothers and two sisters.

We had the first lesson today. I read him a story by Anton Chekhov and then I tried to get him to repeat words, but in the end he said he just liked being read to – it's more restful I think. So that's what I did. I'm going to show him the photographs that I took at Livadia. Mama, Ania, Olga and Tatiana are proper nurses now, with certificates. Olga and Tatiana have to thread needles and hand instruments at operations and yesterday Tatiana had to cut a cast from a man's leg. This evening, while Shura was brushing my hair, I wrote a letter to Papa.

November 8th

Two soldiers in our hospital died today. And only yesterday Marie and I were sitting and chatting to them. I helped Alexis build a bonfire and he smeared ashes all over his face, as camouflage, he said. He's completely obsessed by soldiers. He's got a uniform now and he plays war games all day long. He even persuaded Pyotr Vasilievich to go to Petrograd to buy him some special spades to dig trenches with! Aunt Ella has come to stay. She's going to inspect the hospitals here to see if there are any improvements she can make to her own hospital in Moscow. Orchie is very ill with pneumonia – Mama says her time may be coming. She's 74, which is pretty old.

December 3rd

Orchie died two days ago. She was buried in the little graveyard in the park and an English priest came and read the service. There was hardly anyone there, apart from us – Orchie only had one sister and she's in England. Mama is sad because she'd known Orchie practically all her life, but I'm not particularly.

December 24th

Papa is home. We helped decorate a Christmas tree for the

men in the big hospital and also in mine and Marie's hospital and then we handed out presents – everyone got either a pair of woollen stockings or a scarf, with a tin of biscuits. And Father Vasilev held a mass.

Of course we had our own trees too, but this year there are no presents. It is a different kind of Christmas, because of the war, but I don't especially mind. In fact I think my life is much more interesting than it was before. It always used to be just lessons and church and visiting relations. Now there are still lessons, but every day I'm in the hospital, talking to the men and helping. Even though I'm not a proper nurse I'm almost one and Mama says that keeping the men cheerful – she calls it boosting their morale – is just as important a job as dressing wounds and things. I think I like being a morale booster.

1915

January 6th

Ania has been in a train crash. She was coming to Tsarskoe Selo, from Petrograd. Her legs were crushed and her back was also hurt. She's been brought to the big hospital here. Papa and Mama have been to see her and they say that she's unconscious and may even die.

January 8th

Our Friend went to see Ania today. Mama told us that he took her hand and called her name and she suddenly opened her eyes. Then he said, 'Now wake up and rise,' and she tried to get up. And when he said 'Speak to me,' she spoke! I don't care what people say about Our Friend – I think that shows he really *can* perform miracles. He says that Ania will get better, but she'll be crippled. Alexis and I walked with Papa this afternoon. Alexis snuck up behind me and threw a snowball when I wasn't looking. Papa said, 'To attack someone when they can't defend themselves is the kind of behaviour you'd expect from a German – you should be ashamed of yourself!' Alexis apologised.

Marie has Becker (our code word for periods), so she's in bed resting. Olga and Tatiana have gone to the Winter Palace to receive donations for the families of the soldiers in their regiments and then they're going to visit hospitals in Petrograd. Mama's heart is bad. Up until Christmas she was so well, but now she hardly ever is.

January 11th

I no longer have to have cold baths – hurray! We have a silver bathtub, hidden behind a curtain in the dressing room, and sometimes I put almond oil in the *lovely warm* water. It feels most luxurious. Marie and I also have proper beds now and we're going to get dressing tables.

January 17th

Marie and I went to visit Ania in the hospital. She says she has a lot of pain, but she can move her legs a bit and she wants to be back in her house. She looks fatter than ever.

February 16th

Had history and arithmetic with Trina – that's what we call Mlle Schneider. Trina never makes me do anything I don't want to, but her lessons are awfully dull. I'm still trying to teach Ivan Petrovich, my soldier, to read and write. I don't think we've made much progress, but he loves being read to and he loves looking at my photograph albums. Usually we just talk. He says thousands and thousands of Russian soldiers are being killed and that there aren't enough weapons or even enough food. Most of the boys he grew up with in his village are dead. He has nearly recovered from his wound, which means he'll have to fight again. He wishes that he'd lost a leg or something, then at least he wouldn't have to go back.

We're learning to shoot – Papa arranged for target soldiers to be put up in the clearing by the big lake and one of the officers who's been in the hospital is teaching us. Of course Alexis spends every minute he can practising. Tatiana is the best of all of us, because she's so careful, while I'm not very good because I get impatient and don't line up properly. I asked Ivan Petrovich if he'd actually shot a German and he said that he'd lost his gun before he got a chance to fire it. I don't think Ivan Petrovich is meant to be a soldier; he just wants to grow grapes in the Crimea.

February 23rd
It's been snowing a lot. Drove to Pavlovsk – the prettiest palace we have I think – with Mama and Marie, for tobogganing in the park. Olga and Tatiana are in Petrograd for committee meetings of some of their charities.

March 11th
As a special treat we were allowed to use Papa's bathtub. It was tremendous fun! Papa's bath is sunk into the floor of

his dressing room and it's so big and deep that it's really more like a swimming pool than a bath. I went on my own first and swam in little circles and then Marie came in too and we fooled around and pushed each other under and the dogs ran around barking like mad. I wrote to Papa to thank him.

March 28th

Felix and Irina's baby was christened yesterday and we all went to Petrograd, to the Yusupov Palace, for the christening. The baby is also called Irina, which Mama thinks is strange, but big Irina says that she loves her name so much she couldn't think of a better one for her daughter and I see what she means. The priest practically drowned little Irina and she screamed her head off.

Afterwards there was a magnificent tea with the most delicious hot chocolate, so thick you practically needed a spoon to drink it. Grandmama was there and all our cousins. I heard Felix saying to my cousin Dmitri that Grigory – he meant Our Friend – had behaved scandalously in a restaurant and had said, about Mama (I'm not sure I heard this right), 'I can make the old girl do anything I like.' Then Dmitri said, 'He's a scoundrel of the first order and something's got to be done about him before he does any more damage.'

Usually I like Dmitri, but not any more. And I know Our Friend would never talk about Mama like that. I told Tatiana and she said on no account to say anything to Mama because it will only upset her.

April 17th

Marie's and my dressing tables arrived today. Irina makes face lotion out of cucumber and sour cream, which she says is very good for keeping your skin soft. She gave me the instructions, so I'm going to ask Shura to help me make some. Mama isn't well, so she's lying on the sofa in her mauve room and Tatiana is reading to her. Tomorrow my sisters and I are going to Petrograd, to the Winter Palace, to give medals to soldiers, for bravery in battle and things. We're going instead of Mama.

April 19th

Giving the medals took ages – there was a huge long line of soldiers and a lot of them had lost a leg or an arm and some of them were in wheelchairs. Shaking hands and smiling all the time was quite tiring, in fact I couldn't wait for it to be over. Tatiana kept poking me in the ribs because I was slouching.

Afterwards we visited a couple of hospitals – more smiling and shaking hands – and then, at last, we went for tea at the Anitchkov with Grandmama. Felix and Irina were there and Felix said that people had thrown stones at Aunt Ella's carriage, in Moscow, and spat at her, all because she's German. Really she's only half German, the same as Mama, and it seems very unfair that people should hate her for something she can't help, especially when she's always working in her hospitals. I hope no one hates Mama.

May 27th

It's beautifully warm now. Marie and I had lessons on the terrace. Mr Gibbes has had a haircut and he's also started wearing a flower – a carnation – in his button hole. I asked him if he had a sweetheart and he blushed bright red and said 'What nonsense you talk, Anastasia Nicolaevna.' So I said 'Oh, Mr Gibbes, my suspicions are confirmed!' Actually I don't think he has a sweetheart at all – he's much too shy and stiff and he never talks to Shura, who's very pretty, or to any of Mama's ladies.

Alexis has been given a toy motor car – it's dark blue and looks exactly like a proper one – and he drives it around the park all day long, honking the horn and annoying everyone.

May 30th

Papa has come home for a few days. He looks very tired and a bit worried I think. He says the war is not going as well as he'd hoped. He came riding with Tatiana and me and we looked for wild raspberries, but it's too early. After dinner he read Turgenev to us while we knitted stockings for the troops. Our Friend was there as well – he doesn't approve of the war and he started muttering things about Russia drowning in her own blood. I could see Papa getting quite exasperated.

June 18th

My fourteenth birthday. Ania has given me a puppy! He's a King Charles spaniel – black and brown, extremely soft and silky and absolutely adorable. I've called him Jimmy. I think he'll be a nice friend for Alexis's spaniel Joy, but I think he might be bullied by Tatiana's Ortino, because Ortino is quite old and grumpy.

I also got a table tennis set from Mama and Papa and Papa sent me a telegram. Otherwise it was an ordinary sort of day – lessons and the hospital and riding with Tatiana. It was warm enough to have lunch on the terrace.

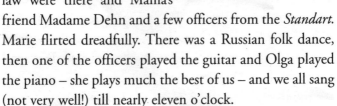

In the evening, after dinner, Olga, Tatiana, Marie and me went to Ania's for a little party. Her brother and sister-in-law were there and Mama's friend Madame Dehn and a few officers from the *Standart*. Marie flirted dreadfully. There was a Russian folk dance, then one of the officers played the guitar and Olga played the piano – she plays much the best of us – and we all sang (not very well!) till nearly eleven o'clock.

I feel quite old now and I really think it's about time that Becker started. I hate being the odd one out, even though Marie says it's a dreadful nuisance and you have to lie down a lot and not do anything.

July 2nd

Ortino snaps at Jimmy whenever Jimmy goes bouncing up

to him, which he does all the time. He is absolutely the sweetest dog in the world. I'm training him, but he still has quite a few accidents, so he's not allowed to sleep in my room yet – he has a kind of pen in the nursery.

I rolled bandages in the stores this afternoon for hours and hours. We went to Ania's after dinner and acted some little plays. Ania still has to use crutches to walk and she probably always will. She doesn't exactly complain, but she definitely wants everyone to feel sorry for her.

July 24th

Yesterday my sisters and I (Mama stayed with Alexis because he's hurt his leg – he banged his knee on something and now it's all swollen) went to Petrograd and had tea at the Anitchkov with Aunt Ella. I asked her about the people who threw stones and she said that it was true and that there will always be ignorant people who hate the innocent. But she also said that so many Russians are being killed that it's only natural that people feel angry and want to blame someone. German bakeries in Petrograd have had their windows smashed.

I wish this war would be over. It was boiling hot in Petrograd and the river stank, so it was very nice to get back to Tsarskoe Selo.

August 8th

Papa is back. He seems very worried and distracted and he keeps having meetings with ministers – he's in his study with General Polivanov, his Minister of War right now –

and talking to Mama for hours. Warsaw has fallen to the Germans, which is bad news I think. Alexis is still in bed. I sat with him and did a puzzle and then Monsieur Gilliard put on a magic lantern show to cheer him up.

August 11th

Papa is to become commander-in-chief of the army instead of Uncle Nikolasha. I've always liked Uncle Nikolasha (he's actually Papa's cousin), even though he can be rather gruff. He's tremendously tall and straight and somehow looks exactly like you'd expect a soldier to look. I asked Papa if he'd thought Uncle Nikolasha wasn't doing a good job, but he said it wasn't that, it was just that he felt that the army needed their Tsar. I'm very proud of him and I'm sure the war will go better now.

Our Friend came in the evening. He's pleased about Uncle Nikolasha going, but then he's never liked Uncle Nikolasha, which I can't help feeling might be because Uncle Nikolasha has always been jolly rude about him. He blessed Papa.

August 12th

Papa left for Stavka – that's what we call military headquarters – yesterday and Mama has gone with him. We walked to Znamenia and lit a big candle for them and for Russia. Then we prayed. I prayed for the war to be over and Papa to be home with us and Mama and Alexis to be well. I also prayed that my legs would grow. Marie and I went to meet our hospital train and later we gave icons to all the men who've just arrived. I have a sore throat – I hope I'm not going to be ill.

August 18th

I've been in bed for five days with influenza, but today I feel better. Marie has been ill too. Dr Botkin came to see us this morning and Marie didn't want him to see her in bed, so she lay with the covers right over her, even though it was perfectly obvious that she was there. When Dr Botkin took off his glasses to polish them (one of his habits) and said, 'Now where has Marie Nicolaevna got to?' (pretending he couldn't see her) I pulled her covers right off. She was terribly embarrassed. After Dr Botkin had gone she tried to tip me out of bed and we both ended up on the floor. I'm getting up tomorrow.

August 20th

Dr Botkin has let me sit out on Mama's balcony. So I'm basking in the sun. Olga has brought a gramophone back from Petrograd and we're going to play it after dinner.

August 29th

The dentist came today. Marie had two fillings and Mama has to have a tooth pulled, but I was lucky and didn't have anything. After lunch Olga, Marie and I drove to Pavlovsk and walked in the park. On the way home we stopped at a little shop and bought some strawberry jam. I've been in our hospital, playing whist with the officers, and now I'm going back there for a Te Deum. One of the officers loves playing his guitar and singing, but there've been some complaints that he makes too much noise, so he's promised to only play quietly.

September 8th

Lessons have started again. Alexis is going to Stavka with Papa, to live for a while, not just to visit. I'm very jealous. It's all because he's a boy. Mama doesn't want to let him go – she worries so – but Papa thinks it'll be good for him and useful training for when he becomes tsar, so she's agreed. And he'll have Monsieur Gilliard and Mr Gibbes, and Derevenko and Nagorny of course. Alexis is completely overexcited and leaping about all over the place.

September 10th

Papa and Alexis left today. It does feel very strange without Alexis – I miss him much more than I thought I would. Mama has been awfully anxious. She never stops writing long letters to him and Papa.

Had literature with Pyotr Vasilievich this morning. We're reading *Childhood, Boyhood, Youth*, by Tolstoy. I asked Pyotr Vaslievich about his son, who he doesn't see any more because he's a Menshevik and he's had to go into exile. I think Mensheviks believe that Russia should be governed by the people not by the Tsar, but as Russia has always had a tsar I don't really see how that could happen.

Marie and I have been putting the cucumber lotion on our faces every night, but it doesn't seem to make much difference and now it's beginning to stink because the cream in going off.

September 26th

Jimmy did the Governor (that's our word for dog mess) right in the middle of the carpet in Olga and Tatiana's room. Luckily I found it before they did. I have a little silver shovel and bucket for clearing it up.

October 17th

I got a letter from Alexis. He sounds very happy. He says that he shares a room with Papa and he's made friends with the officers – they play football with him. I wish I was at Stavka, though I would miss my hospital. We never go anywhere now. Olga has asked Mama if she can have a room of her own – she says that now she's 21 and grown up she doesn't want to share with Tatiana any more. Mama has said no and now Olga is sulking. Tatiana is cross with Olga for bothering Mama. I'm on Olga's side – I'd like my own room too and in my view Tatiana is simply a goody goody.

October 26th

Went to confession with Father Vasilev. Olga is ill. Mama says that she's been working too hard in the hospital and at her charity committees and things and that she's got overtired and nervous. We had dinner upstairs in the nursery, so Olga could join us.

November 3rd

It rained all day. Had history with Trina this morning. I've grown quite fond of Trina. She's very shy – the absolute opposite of Sovanna, and me – so it takes a long time to feel you know her. Although her name sounds German she's actually French. She's rather plump – in fact everything about her is round, even her hair which she wears in a sort of fat bun – which isn't surprising because she has a terribly sweet tooth. She's always sucking raspberry bonbons that she gets sent from France and she says Russians have no idea how to make desserts.

In the afternoon I went to read to Ivan Petrovich for the last time, because he's leaving the hospital tomorrow to go back to the war. It was extremely sad saying goodbye. He says that he's happy to die for Russia, but I don't think he really wants to fight at all. I gave him an icon which I hope will keep him safe and I lit a candle for him at Znamenia.

Olga is better, but she's not working in the hospital yet. She's still angry with Mama about the room. In fact Olga's always bad tempered these days. We think she might have a broken heart – the officer, on the *Standart*, who she liked last summer, has got married. Olga says she doesn't mind, but Marie says they'd been writing to each other. Of course Olga could never have married him.

November 12th

I've got Becker! I realised this afternoon, after I'd been skating and I had a bad stomach pain. When I told Mama she cried a little and said, 'I can't believe that all my girlies are grown up.' Shura gave me what I need – a sort of belt and strips of padded cloth. It feels very uncomfortable and embarrassing, but exciting too. I rested in bed until dinner.

November 27th

It snowed a lot yesterday. Went tobogganing at Pavlovsk with Marie. It's the first snow that Jimmy's ever seen and he kept dipping his nose in it and then shaking his head in a puzzled kind of way. I'm training him to sit on his hind legs and beg – he gets a sugar lump as a reward.

We saw Our Friend at Ania's. When we were leaving he blessed us and said, 'The path is narrow, but one must walk along it straight in the manner of God and not of man,' which sounds very wise I think.

December 6th

Papa is bringing Alexis back to Tsarskoe Selo because he has a nosebleed which won't stop.

December 9th

Alexis is back. He looked very pale when he arrived and he had bandages all around his face. Our Friend came to see him. Mama told us how he stood by Alexis's bed and made the sign of the cross and said, 'Don't be alarmed. Nothing will happen.' Then he just walked out of the room and Alexis fell asleep. By this morning the bleeding had stopped and now he's much better. Papa has gone back to Stavka.

December 18th

Sat with Alexis – he still has to stay in bed – and played patience for ages. He's furious because the doctors say he won't be able to go to Stavka for months.

1916

January 3rd

Olga and I went sledging in the really fast sleigh with three horses. Alexis was given a diary for Christmas and he's very funny about it. He writes it in advance – at lunchtime he describes the evening and sometimes even the next day. He says it saves time. He was also given some toy pistols, which we kept firing all through dinner until Mama made us stop. Knitted stockings after dinner while Olga read aloud.

January 29th

Haven't written this for ages because I've been in bed with bronchitis. I don't have a temperature any more and Dr Botkin has let me get up, but I have to stay upstairs. I looked in the mirror this morning – a repulsive sight. My face is all green and my hair is all limp and greasy. I think

I'm thinner though – a good thing! Alexis has been ill too, which at least has been company. And Mama's heart has been very bad. So we really are a family of invalids. Mama couldn't come upstairs to see me when I was ill, so we sent each other little notes and sometimes talked on the telephone. But she came today.

Marie told me that cousin Boris – his father is Papa's uncle, Grand Duke Vladimir, which is rather complicated – proposed to Olga! Mama was furious and said she'd never let Olga marry a man with such a dreadful reputation and low morals and so much older too – he's about 40.

February 12th

There's a new officer in our hospital – Andrei Vasilievich Shuvalov. He was shot in the arm in Galicia, fighting the Austrians, and he was also gassed. His arm will probably have to be amputated. He's 22 and I think he's very handsome – he has a thin face and grey eyes and a beautiful smile. I sat with him and chatted and he told me that his father has a small estate near Moscow which he hopes to inherit one day as he's the eldest son. His father was a friend of Tolstoy, Papa's favourite writer. His mother died, of cholera, when he was only seven and then he was looked after by his mother's old governess, who was English – a bit like Orchie. He went to Paris to study and he's also been to England to learn about new ways of farming. Tonight we're going to perform a play for the men in the big hospital. It's called *The Distorting Mirror.*

February 19th

Went tobogganing with Marie and Olga – the snow mountain is absolutely enormous now.

February 22nd

Worked in the stores with Marie and our cousin Maria. We rolled bandages and sorted out clothes and fooled around a lot. I put on some men's trousers and a jacket and Marie drew a moustache on me and then I went out to serve people like that, until Tatiana arrived and made me change. Andrei Vasilievich had his arm amputated yesterday.

February 23rd

Tatiana told Mama about me dressing up in men's clothes, which is absolutely swinish of her. So of course I got a talking-to. Mama said all the usual things about being the Tsar's daughter and how people looked up to us and setting an example and how shocked Papa would be by such vulgar behaviour and how I was a young lady of nearly fifteen, not a clown, etc etc. Now I can't work in the stores for two weeks. And it was just a joke! Sometimes I think Mama is ridiculous.

March 28th

We went to a concert in the big hospital last night. Olga got in a grump because Mama made her change out of her nurse's uniform. The stars of the evening were twin boy dwarfs, who did a Russian dance. They couldn't get through the audience, to the stage, so the soldiers lifted them up and passed them over their heads!

This afternoon I played bezique with Andrei Vasilievich. I asked him if he had a sweetheart and he told me that before the war he met an English girl, who was the daughter of some friends of his father's, but that now she was in England and he didn't know if he'd ever see her again.

Some of the officers from our hospital are going to the Crimea to convalesce. I wish I was going with them. I suppose we won't be able to go to Livadia until after the war is over, but I think a lot about waking up and being able to see the sea from my bed, and warm sand, and the smell of roses and pines. And I wish I was thinner and not so lumpy, and that my nose wasn't so long and my legs weren't so short and my hair wasn't boring mousy brown. In fact I wish that I was as tall and thin as Tatiana and that I had Marie's blue eyes and gold hair and that I was as clever and good at dancing as Olga. Then I'd be perfect! Mama is having her face electrified – it's to help the pains in her face.

April 11th

Started painting eggs for Easter. I have a pimple right on the end of my nose.

April 21st

Easter. We went to the midnight service at Znamenia, which was very beautiful. Very busy all day handing out eggs in the hospitals. Every soldier got an egg – and that's a lot of eggs. Then there was a Te Deum. I also managed to eat masses of kulich and paskha and now I'm as fat as a pig. We missed Papa very much – he sent Mama her Faberge egg. The weather is boiling.

May 18th

It's still incredibly hot. Marie and I have moved our beds out from behind the screens and put them right under the window. We had lessons on the terrace. Aunt Olga and our cousin Dmitri came for tea. Dmitri was as funny as usual – he even makes Mama laugh and that's something that doesn't happen very often these days. He asked Marie how many new boyfriends she had this week. Aunt Olga has asked Papa for permission to get divorced from Uncle Petia so she can marry someone else. Mama says it's an absolute disgrace, even though she loves Aunt Olga, and that the Tsar's family should be setting an example to the rest of society.

People do seem to get divorced quite a lot in our family (hope I don't). Maybe it's catching. But in my view Aunt Olga should be allowed to marry the person she loves. She hardly ever seemed to see Uncle Petia anyway so she couldn't have liked him very much. We spent the evening in the big hospital. Olga and Tatiana cleaned instruments and Marie and I chatted with the men and played cards and Mama did a puzzle. It was very cosy. We're all going to go to Stavka in a few days, to see Papa, which is most exciting.

May 26th, Mogilev

We've been at Stavka for five days now. We're living in train carriages which are parked in a kind of circle in the forest. They're quite comfortable. We go and have lunch in the Governor's house, with Papa's staff and various officers. Alexis is delighted to be back – he knows everyone and he's very popular.

Papa is busy all morning, but after lunch we all motor to somewhere near the Dnieper river. Then we go for a long walk along the river with Papa, while Mama stays near the cars and rests. Dmitri and Fat Orlov and some of the officers come for dinner in our carriage and we play cards and have a very merry time. Sometimes, in the evening, we watch cinema films of the war (quite dull), and also episodes of *The Mysterious Hand*, which is a murder mystery (much more fun). Count Fredericks is here as well, but he's so deaf now and so forgetful that it's quite hard to have a conversation with him. He thought I was Tatiana.

May 28th

This morning we girls went to visit some of the peasants' cottages nearby and played with the children. We brought them some little presents and sweets. They were quite shy at first, but then they didn't want to let us go. After lunch we took the steamboat along the river for a while. Then we moored and made a fire and baked potatoes.

June 1st, Tsarskoe Selo

We got home yesterday, which I'm quite sorry about, though I do look forward to going to our hospital and seeing everyone. It was boiling hot on the journey and whenever the train stopped my sisters and I lay outside on the little platform at the back and sunned ourselves. Mama was very disapproving, but we took no notice and now we're all quite brown!

Alexis has stayed at Stavka. Ania brought Our Friend to drink tea with us – we haven't seen him for ages. He looked at me in the way he does, as if he's looking inside you, and said, 'Ah, my little Anastasia, not so little any more! I know the secrets of your heart!' I just managed to stop myself from telling him that he didn't.

June 9th

Tatiana, Marie and I rowed around the big lake until we got gobbled by mosquitoes and had to stop. Then we sat on the bank and kept the mosquitoes away by smoking the cigarettes that Papa gave us.

June 24th

Marie and I weeded our hospital garden and then we played croquet with the officers. I played with Andrei Vasilievich. Most of his shots went completely wide – it's not easy playing croquet with one arm. Even so we didn't do too badly.

Marie kept asking the men to show her how to hold her mallet, but when I told her to stop flirting she got very cross and said she wasn't flirting and anyway what about me and Andrei Vasilievich. But that's different – we're friends. Ania is having one of her little parties this evening. I don't really want to go as I find them awfully dull these days, but Mama says I must.

June 25th

Ania's party was as dull as usual. Her mother and father were there and Madame Dehn and her husband, who has a silly laugh, and we had to sit and listen to a Rumanian band for hours. There was lots of talk about the war – even though Papa is doing everything he can, the government is making a muddle of things and people are protesting.

I went to meet the hospital train this afternoon – it was just bursting with soldiers, mostly in a dreadful state. I walked around and talked to some of them and tried to say something cheerful, which really is quite difficult. They're going to start building a new hospital as more and more wounded arrive all the time and there simply isn't room.

July 17th

Mama has gone to spend a few days with Papa at Stavka. Olga and Tatiana are in town, receiving donations and having committee meetings. Marie and I have just got back from a Te Deum in our hospital.

I had a long talk with Andrei Vasilievich yesterday. He said that there are lots of bad rumours about Our Friend and people feel that he has too much influence on Mama. Some people are even saying that he's a spy for the Germans! I tried to explain how Our Friend helps us and especially Mama and Alexis (I think Andrei Vasilievich knew what I meant, even though we're not supposed to talk about Alexis's illness). Then I said what Mama always tells us, about how saints have always been persecuted, but even as I was saying it I wondered if it was really true. Nobody seems to think Our Friend is a good man except for us and Ania. I know Andrei Vasilievich likes Mama, so I think he must be really worried.

I asked Andrei about what they were saying at Ania's, about the government being bad. He said that he didn't think some of Papa's ministers were the best men to be governing Russia, particularly during the war and with Papa away at Stavka, and that Russia needs a government that people trust and that has the support of the Duma*. I told him that I thought Papa would be very interested to hear his opinion, but he just laughed and said, 'I'm sure the Tsar has more important things on his mind,' and asked me to tell him one of my jokes. I sometimes wonder if he thinks I'm pretty at all.

August 3rd

Mama isn't well – she's lying on her balcony and Tatiana is reading to her. Marie and I have been working in the stores.

September 10th

Aunt Ella arrived from Moscow yesterday to see Mama. She went straight to Mama's mauve room, and she'd only been there for about an hour before Mama rang the bell and ordered a carriage to take her back to the station. Then she left without even having seen us! It was very strange. When I asked Mama why she'd left like that – usually she stays with us for at least a week – Mama's face went all tight and she just said that she and Aunt Ella couldn't see eye to eye about some things. But Olga and Tatiana say that it's all to do with Our Friend, so I immediately thought about my talk with Andrei Vasilievich. Aunt Ella is so holy and good – you'd think she'd understand about Our Friend.

October 17th

We all went to town with Mama, to visit the hospital in the Winter Palace and to give out medals. Mama had to be carried up the stairs and then wheeled in her chair. There was a group of very angry-looking people waiting when we came out of the palace to get into the motor. One of them, a man, pointed at Mama and said 'There goes the Nemka!' which means 'German woman'. And a woman shouted, 'Our children are starving – give us bread!' Mama just said to take no notice, but they did look awfully thin and tired. Then some policemen rushed up and shooed them away.

It's so unfair that people call Mama German – it's not her fault that she was born in Germany and she's lived in Russia for years and years and she feels completely Russian and not a bit German and anyway she hates Uncle Willy.

When we got back to Tsarskoe Selo I told Andrei Vasilievich about what had happened. He thinks that wars make people prejudiced and anyone with German blood is bound to be disliked – it's nothing to do with Mama personally. When I asked him about the woman and the bread he said that people are terribly short of food in the cities because the railways aren't working properly and supplies aren't getting through. He said the government needed to do something about it. I think I'll write to Papa about this.

November 3rd

Aunt Olga is getting married tomorrow, so we sent her a telegram. Her new husband is called Nicholas Kulikovsky and he's an officer. He's come back from the front for the wedding. I do hope he doesn't get killed.

November 11th

Papa has come home for a few days. He looks very tired and quite old I think – he's got grey hairs now and lots of wrinkles. And Crown Prince Carol of Rumania, the one who wanted to marry Olga, is here. This time he wants to marry Marie! I said he can't have really been in love with Olga if he's switched to Marie so easily. She's not even eighteen anyway. Papa has told him it's impossible.

Last night there was a big dinner for Prince Carol and Marie went (as usual I wasn't allowed because I'm still too young). Marie wore a light blue dress and her birthday diamonds and she was terribly excited, not because of Prince Carol – even Marie wouldn't flirt with Prince Carol – but because we hardly ever dress up these days. But when she came to bed later – I'd stayed awake on purpose – she told me that when she was walking down the steps into the banqueting hall she'd tripped in her heels and fallen flat on her face in front of everybody! She's still blushing now.

November 12th

I asked Papa why so many people disapprove of Our Friend and he sighed and said, 'People misunderstand Grigory, but really he's a simple, honest soul. Besides, you know how he calms Mama's nerves – that's a great thing.' Then I said, 'So he doesn't do bad things?' And Papa gave me an anxious look and asked me what I meant. I couldn't explain.

November 19th

Someone has poisoned Ania's dachshund Boris! She found him near her house, just by the path that goes down to the small lake. She thinks it's because dachshunds are German – well of course they're not really, but the war has made people go crazy. I can hardly believe it. Poor Ania's in a dreadful state, and so would I be if someone had poisoned Jimmy, though the truth is Boris wasn't exactly the nicest dog, being dreadfully smelly and yappy.

November 24th, Mogilev

We've come to Stavka to be with Papa. It's somehow not as

much fun as last time. Papa seems distracted. He and Mama spend hours talking on their own in their carriage and then seem quite cross with each other. Normally, they're never cross. Olga says they're arguing about Protopopov, who's a minister in the government. Papa thinks he's not very good at his job and Mama thinks he is. Also Fat Orlov has been sent away because he was telling horrid stories about Our Friend and, even though he shouldn't have done that, I do quite miss him – he was always so jolly. Only Alexis seems really happy.

December 11th, Tsarskoe Selo

We've been on another trip, to Novgorod, which is one of the most ancient and holy towns in Russia. We went on the train and Ania came with us. She complained all the way about pains in her legs. She has an annoying way of saying, 'Oh, don't pay any attention to me, dears,' when you know that what she really wants is lots of attention!

When we arrived we went to a service in the cathedral and then to a hospital, where we walked around and gave icons to the wounded. Then we went to an old monastery where there's a famous staritsa – that's a holy woman. She's 107 years old but her face has hardly any wrinkles. She was lying in bed, in a tiny room, and even though she never washes she didn't smell at all. Mama went in first and we heard the staritsa say, 'Behold the martyred Empress Alexandra Fodorovna!', which seemed quite odd as Mama isn't a martyr. She said a few more words to Mama and gave her an apple to give to Papa. Then we girls went in and she made the sign of the cross and said, 'You will marry,' and told us to come and see her again. Then she spoke to Ania. Mama said she made her feel very peaceful, but I don't feel any different – it's nice to know we'll find husbands though!

December 13th

One of the officers in our hospital has been sent away because he was making fun of our journey to Novgorod – he said that the people there had to be bribed to come out and cheer for us because no one supports Papa any more. I think that's horrible and it's not true anyway.

This afternoon Olga, Tatiana and I went tobogganing. Marie has Becker. Then we went with Mama to Ania's house for tea and saw Our Friend. Ania says that he hardly ever goes out any more, as he's had threatening letters and he's worried that someone might try and kill him, like the woman who stabbed him.

December 17th

Our Friend has disappeared. At dinner yesterday Ania said that he had told her he was going to the Yusupov Palace that evening to meet Irina, which Mama thought was rather odd as she knew Irina was in the Crimea. Now there are rumours that the police heard shots last night, coming from the Yusupov Palace, though they say it was just someone shooting a dog. Mama has been telephoning and says we can only pray and trust to God, but Ania thinks something bad has happened.

December 18th

Our Friend has been *murdered* and they're saying that Felix and Dmitri did it! His body has been found in the Neva and he'd been shot. I think there were a couple of other men who helped Felix and Dmitri, but apparently Felix fired the gun. I can't believe it. Felix is Irina's husband and Dmitri is our cousin – how could they do such a thing? I'm not going to be able to sleep tonight – Marie and I are going to stay in Olga and Tatiana's room. Tatiana is going to stay with Mama. Mama has been crying terribly. She keeps saying, 'Who will save Baby now?' and 'What will become of Russia?' Papa is on his way home.

December 21st

Our Friend was buried today, in the park. It was just us and Ania and Papa's minister, Protopopov. We put an icon, from Novgorod, in the coffin, which we'd signed on the back. Father Vasilev read the service and then we threw flowers onto the coffin as it was put into the ground. Mama was very brave. A church is going to be built over the grave. After lunch Olga, Marie and I went for a walk with Papa and he explained a bit about what had happened. He said that Felix and Dmitri believed that they were helping Russia by killing Our Friend, but it's still murder and they have to be punished. He said we've all got to try and comfort Mama because it's hardest for her – she relied so on Our Friend. Everything is horrible.

December 22nd

Uncle Sandro came to see Papa yesterday. We could hear him shouting in Papa's study. Later Papa told us that Uncle Sandro had asked him not to punish Felix and Dmitri. Apparently everyone in the family – Uncle Pavel, Aunt Olga, Aunt Ella, even Grandmama – think they should be forgiven. But Papa says that the fact that it was members of our own family who killed Our Friend just makes it worse. I agree.

Felix and Dmitri are to be exiled. I remember hearing them talking at little Irina's christening – perhaps if I'd told Papa then they would have been stopped. It seems that they tricked Our Friend and gave him some poisoned cakes and wine and when that didn't work Felix shot him. That's just wicked. Then I keep thinking about Irina and how her husband is a murderer.

Tatiana says that Irina knew that Felix was plotting to kill Our Friend and that she supported him because she thought it would save Papa – how could she think that?

104

What could she mean? Nothing makes sense.

December 23rd

I can't stop thinking about what's happened. One minute I start wondering whether maybe Our Friend wasn't such a good man – he could make you feel a bit uncomfortable and I've never forgotten seeing him with Shura, and just about everybody, apart from us, seemed to hate him. And then I think that doesn't mean that he deserved to be murdered and anyway if he hadn't been a true Man of God how could he have saved Alexis's life? But maybe he sort of tricked Mama and Papa. Mama is so desperate for Alexis to be well that it makes her quite unreasonable and Papa is so good that perhaps he can't see bad in other people.

December 27th

It hasn't been an awfully jolly Christmas. We did trees for the hospitals and handed out presents to the men, but we didn't exchange presents with the uncles and aunts and cousins. I don't think anyone felt very cheerful or Christmassy, except Alexis perhaps, even though his wrist is hurting him and he's in bed. This afternoon Papa came skating with Tatiana, Marie and me and now we're all sitting in Mama's mauve room doing the map of Russia puzzle that Grandmama sent.

1917

January 1st

Last night, during the New Year Te Deum, I prayed like mad for the war to be over and Mama and Alexis to be well and everything to be alright. Ania has come to live with us in the Alexander Palace because she's had horrible letters and Mama thinks it's not safe for her to be in her house.

January 9th

Tobogganed down the snow mountain with Marie and Alexis (he's better). In the evening Marie and I went to our hospital and served tea and played cards with the men. Andrei Vasilievich is leaving in a few days' time – he's going to go to his father's estate until the war is over and then he hopes to travel and maybe to study more. He also wants to make improvements on his father's estate – to build new houses and a school for the peasants and teach them how to grow better crops.

I told him about Felix and Dmitri and how everyone seems worried and sad and he said that these are very difficult times for Russia and that there need to be some changes. I asked him what sort of changes, but he just looked rather uncomfortable and said, 'Oh, people are unhappy with the government.' I told him I'd miss our talks, and he said so would he and he'd send me a card from Moscow. The English ambassador is having a meeting with Papa in his study.

January 23rd

Uncle Sandro came for lunch. He said that Felix and Irina are in the Crimea – Felix has to stay there as punishment – and they're both well. It doesn't sound as if Felix is very sorry.

At the end of lunch Uncle Sandro started talking about politics. He said that there's got to be a government that the Duma supports and that all our family think the same. Papa didn't say anything, but Mama snapped, 'You seem to forget that Nicky doesn't have to answer to anyone but God – why on earth should he be dictated to by that rabble?' (I think she meant the Duma). Uncle Sandro said, 'Please Alix, can we go and talk about this calmly in your room?' They were in there for ages and it sounded like they were arguing. Uncle Sandro looked angry when he left and barely said goodbye to us – I do wish he wouldn't come and upset everyone. Mama had to go and lie down because her heart pains started. After dinner we sat cosily in her sitting room and Papa read aloud while we knitted.

February 2nd

Uncle Misha – he's Papa's younger brother – has come to visit us. We haven't seen him for ages, mostly because Papa and Mama won't receive his wife – she was divorced and Uncle Misha married her without Papa's permission. The great thing about Uncle Misha is he's always in a good mood and at the moment it's just nice to see someone cheery. He's very handsome and he's mad about motor cars.

February 15th

Shura told me that in Petrograd people are breaking into bakeries to steal bread and the factory workers are on strike. It's never been so cold – minus 29. Papa, Tatiana, Marie and I drove to Pavlovsk and had tremendous tobogganing. When we came home Michael Rodzianko, the President of the Duma, was waiting to see Papa.

February 22nd

Papa left today to go back to Stavka. Walked to Znamenia to light candles.

February 24th

Everyone has got measles! Well, nearly everyone. Yesterday Olga and Alexis started coughing and getting spots. Then today Tatiana and Ania did the same. Shura has got it too and Monsieur Gilliard is ill, though he's got influenza not measles. Alexis was playing with some boys from the naval academy a few days ago and one of them had the infection, so Mama thinks that's how it started.

Anyway they're all in bed, and Mama has put on her nurse's uniform and Marie and I are in uniforms made from white summer skirts and dressing gowns. We've got to help because there are so many patients!

Mama also thinks it's better if we catch measles too. We have our meals upstairs in the schoolroom. Ania's room is on the other side of the palace, so Mama has to be wheeled in her chair to go and see her.

February 25th

Olga, Tatiana and Alexis are all in the green bedroom – we call it the measles ward. The curtains are kept drawn, because the light makes their heads worse, so you have to grope around rather. Olga and Tatiana have very high temperatures, but Alexis isn't so bad. Mr Gibbes is reading him *Robinson Crusoe*. Marie and I run around all day helping Mama and Dr Botkin – fetching sponges and towels and water and medicine and answering the telephone.

Actually I'm quite enjoying being a nurse and for once Marie and I don't feel like the youngest. And Tatiana can't be in charge! I do feel sorry for Tatiana though – she's dreadfully ill and she can hardly speak.

This afternoon Mama, Marie and I went to put flowers on Our Friend's grave. There's a church being built over the grave and it's already quite big. We prayed there together. Mama's friend Lili Dehn has come to help us. She's sleeping on a sofa in the red drawing room. She says that everyone in Petrograd is on strike.

February 27th

I think something's happened – Mama keeps telephoning and sending telegrams and having meetings with Count Benckendorff – he's head of the court now instead of Count Fredericks – and she's awfully distracted and nervous. I asked her if anything was the matter, but she said no, there was nothing to worry about and God would take care of us, which is what she always says about everything. Apparently Papa is on his way home.

It's been snowing non-stop, so I sat in the drawing room all afternoon with Lili and Marie, doing a puzzle. As it was getting dark we looked out of the window and saw a big gun, which had been put in the courtyard and lots of soldiers stamping their feet and warming themselves around braziers. I asked Lili what was going on and she said, 'Oh, there's been some trouble in Petrograd – some troops have mutinied.' So I said, 'But why are there all these soldiers *here*?' She said it was just to be on the safe side. Papa will be astonished to find them when he gets home. I do hope he comes soon.

February 28th

Yesterday evening Mama made me go to bed early because I've started coughing (please don't let me be ill). I couldn't sleep and then I heard sounds from outside, so I went to the window and through the darkness I could just see Mama and Marie, all wrapped up in their furs, walking past the lines of soldiers in front of the palace. Count Benckendorff was there too. It was about eleven o'clock and it was still snowing, so I couldn't imagine what they were doing.

When Marie came up to bed, I pounced on her and said, 'What were you and Mama doing out in the dark?' And she said that Mama had suddenly decided it would be a good idea to go and speak to the soldiers, to keep up their morale, and Marie had insisted on going with her. Count Benckendorff had tried to stop them, but in the end he went as well. Mama told Marie just to say something encouraging to each of the men, but Marie couldn't think what to say, except that she hoped they weren't too cold. She heard Mama say, 'The life of the Tsarevich is in your hands' and 'We know we can depend on you', over and over again. Marie thought some of the soldiers looked quite unfriendly and grumpy and she suddenly felt very scared – in fact she says it was the scariest thing she's ever had to do.

For once I don't wish that I'd been there too. After that neither of us could sleep a wink and later we heard gunfire. I don't think Mama went to bed at all – she came in to check on us in the middle of the night and she was still dressed. Now I think I'm definitely getting measles – I've found some spots, though I haven't told anyone yet.

March 16th

So much has happened – I don't know where to begin. I've been ill with measles since the last time I wrote this and today is the first day I've been allowed out of bed. I'm sitting in an armchair in the playroom. Anyway, there's been a revolution which means everything has changed, but the biggest thing of all is that PAPA IS NO LONGER TSAR AND WE'RE ALL PRISONERS! Just writing that seems so strange and unreal. Now I'm going to try and describe everything in the right order.

I can't remember much about when I was first ill, except Mama and Dr Botkin coming in – I was in the green bedroom with Olga and Tatiana. It was always dark. Jimmy slept on my bed the whole time. Once there was a Te Deum in our room and Father Vasilev walked through carrying an icon.

After a few days, I'm not sure how long, but I was feeling a little better, Mama came and sat on the end of Tatiana's bed and said that she had something very difficult to tell us and we had to be extremely brave. She explained that there had been an uprising in Petrograd and some troops had joined in and they'd taken over the Winter Palace and the government had fallen. Now there's a new government – it's called the Provisional Government.

While this was happening Papa was trying to come home to us, but his train was stopped by soldiers, who were revolutionaries, at Pskov. After he'd talked to his generals he decided to abdicate, because he thought that was the only way that Russia could carry on fighting the war and beat the Germans. He wanted Uncle Misha to be tsar instead, but Uncle Misha refused. So now there's no tsar at all. I'm going to stop now and carry on tomorrow because my headache has come back.

March 17th

When Mama was telling us all this I could hardly understand, because of feeling ill. And Tatiana has developed an abscess in her ear, so she couldn't hear a word that Mama was saying and Marie had to write it down for her!

Marie came to sit with us later, and told us that not long after I'd got measles the soldiers who'd come to guard the Alexander Palace had started deserting and then the water and electricity had been cut off (which is why I remember it being so dark) and Count Fredericks's house had been burned down, though he and his wife are alright. Mama kept sending telegrams to Papa, but he didn't reply and the telegrams came back with 'Address of person mentioned unknown' written on them, which made her worry terribly (she didn't know then that his train had been stopped). Marie said that she got more and more frightened, but she felt she had to help Mama all she could. Considering she's not a very brave person, I think she probably was jolly brave. And then Uncle Pavel arrived and he told Mama about Papa abdicating.

Afterwards, Mama told Marie and burst into tears, so of course Marie did as well. But Mama couldn't bear to tell Alexis, so she asked Monsieur Gilliard to do it for her.

Marie said Alexis was very quiet afterwards and kept asking her if Papa would be tsar again one day, and if there wasn't a tsar who would rule Russia? And then Marie got the measles.

A few days later – I think it was March 9th – Papa finally came home. He came straight up to see us in our room, where we were all (except Alexis) still in bed. We were very, very happy to see him. He didn't say very much, just that he loved us and that he'd had to make a very difficult decision, but it was for the good of Russia. He explained that the Provisional Government – that's the new government – has decided to put us under arrest, but it's only until we can go somewhere else, perhaps the Crimea, or even England. It means that we can't leave the Alexander Palace.

Since Papa has been here we've all been feeling better, except for Marie who's still very ill. When Dr Botkin comes to see us, he has a guard with him. The guard doesn't actually come into the room, but he stands at the door and stares at us. Mama is burning her papers and letters.

March 20th

I'm nearly better from the measles, but now I've got bad earache, like Tatiana. I spend most of the day upstairs, sitting in the schoolroom, with Olga and Tatiana. Papa and Mama join us for meals. Alexis comes in and out and entertains us. We spent the morning moulding bullets out of tin – one of Alexis's favourite occupations – with

Monsieur Gilliard. In some ways everything feels normal and in others it doesn't at all. Out of the window you can see sentries all around the palace and you can hear guards tramping up and down the stairs and laughing and singing. We can only use the telephone in the guard room, which is by the round hall, and all our letters get read. The doors of the palace are kept locked and when Papa wants to go out for exercise with Alexis, he has to ask for permission. Even then he can't go very far and guards follow him.

Still Papa seems quite cheerful – he told us how he'd gone for a bicycle ride and a soldier had stuck a bayonet in his wheel and made him fall over, but he just laughed about it. I think Alexis minds more. Papa and Mama keep saying that we must try and remain in good spirits, because although this is a difficult time for us all, it's only until we can go to England. That's where the new government wants to send us. The King of England is Papa's cousin and Papa is very fond of him – everyone says they look like twins. And Mama spent lots of time in England, with Great Granny, when she was a girl. I've been there once, when I was eight, and we sailed on the *Standart* to somewhere called the Isle of Wight and met King Edward – that's the father of George V, who's the King now – on his yacht. King Edward was extremely fat and jolly and Queen Alexandra – she's our grandmama's sister – was extremely thin and pretty, but she could hardly hear anything you said to her because she's terribly deaf.

I don't remember an awful lot about England, except

that everything seemed very small and the teas were delicious, but I wouldn't mind going to live there, as long we could come back to Russia when everything is normal again.

March 21st

Most of the ladies and gentlemen in Papa and Mama's suite have left the palace. I suppose they didn't want to be prisoners. These are the people who've decided to stay with us – Count Benckendorff and his wife, Prince Valia Dolgorukov, Countess Hendrikov, Trina, Dr Botkin and Monsieur Gilliard. And of course Ania and Lili are here. Count Benckendorff still insists on calling Papa 'the Emperor'.

Today, at lunch, Papa said, 'My dear Count, I'm afraid I'm no longer an Emperor, I'm only an ex–Emperor!' Now it's been turned into a joke and even Mama laughs when we say, 'You're only an Ex.'

March 22nd

I'm allowed to come downstairs now, though I still can't go outside. My ears are a lot better. Yesterday a man called Alexander Kerensky came to see us. He's the Minister of Justice in the Provisional Government. We were having lunch in the schoolroom when Count Benckendorff came and told us that he'd arrived. We all felt quite nervous, because we didn't know what he wanted. But when he came in he seemed almost as nervous as we were! He looked more like someone who works in a factory than a minister – he was wearing a very plain shirt buttoned up to the neck, with no collar or cuffs and big boots. And he doesn't have a beard.

He didn't seem to know what to do at first, but then he walked up to Papa, held out his hand and said, in a very brisk kind of way, 'Kerensky'. He shook hands with Mama as well, though you could see she didn't really want to, and she kept biting her lip. He said, 'I've come to inspect the palace and see how you live,' and asked us how we all were – apparently the King and Queen of England are most anxious to hear news of us. Then he and Papa went off for a talk on their own, while we waited in the schoolroom.

But the worst thing Kerensky did was to arrest Ania and Lili! I can't think why – what on earth could they have done? He asked to be shown to Ania's room, where she was in bed – she'd been burning letters and things in the fireplace which probably looked a bit suspicious – and he insisted that she get up and dress. She and Lili were allowed to come and say goodbye to us. They both cried and so did Mama. We all stood and watched them go from the schoolroom window. Poor Ania can still hardly walk, so she hobbled to the car on her crutches. Then they were driven away.

Mama is very angry with Kerensky about this. She keeps saying, 'How could he treat a sick woman like that ? – it's inhuman.' Papa says that Kerensky was so nervous when he was talking to him that he kept twisting Papa's ivory paper knife until Papa had to ask him to put it down because he thought it might snap! He told Papa that we could be sure that the new government would take care of us.

March 24th

A parcel from Aunt Olga arrived today. But when it was given to Mama she found that it had been opened already. There were some tubes of toothpaste that had been ripped open and some chocolate bars that someone had taken great bites from – I suppose it's the guards. Count Benckendorff went to speak to them and he was told that they had orders to inspect anything that was sent to us. Do they really think there might be a bomb in a tube of toothpaste?

I was in the schoolroom this afternoon, playing patience with Tatiana and Countess Hendrikov, when we looked out of the window and saw a guard sitting on one of the gold chairs from the hall, with his feet up on a footstool and his rifle on the ground. He was reading the newspaper and he looked extremely comfortable! It was such a funny sight that we called Papa to come and have a look – he laughed and said, 'Well, that's revolutionary soldiers for you.'

March 25th

It seems that we're not going to England after all. I'm not sure why. I don't mind very much as I'd really rather stay in Russia and perhaps we'll be allowed to go to Livadia instead, but Papa and Mama are upset. In fact Mama seems awfully depressed. She spends most of the day lying on the sofa in her mauve room and she's always saying things like 'It's God who's sent us this ordeal'.

I do wish Mama would stop bringing God into everything – maybe it makes her feel better, but it doesn't me. I mean why *has* he sent us this ordeal? What have we done wrong? Of course I believe in God but sometimes my belief slips rather. I suppose I'm just not religious in the same way as Mama and Olga. Olga prays more than ever these days.

March 27th

When we came out of mass this morning we found that Kerensky had come to see us again. This time he asked to see Mama on her own. Later she told us that he'd asked her lots of questions about whether she'd told Papa to appoint ministers and if she'd helped the Germans at all (how ridiculous), but he'd been perfectly polite. Then he said that Papa and Mama have to be separated – Papa can only join Mama for meals and prayers and then they can only speak Russian and there has to be an officer in the room.

Papa and Mama say it's best just to agree to whatever Kerensky wants, but it feels all wrong to me – Papa was the *Tsar*, well he still is in my view, and he's never had to obey anybody in his life and now suddenly he's being ordered about by someone we'd never even heard of until a few days ago.

April 2nd

Today was Easter Sunday. Considering how much I've

always loved Easter it was not a very joyful day, even though Papa and Mama did their best to make it as normal as possible. The midnight service was in the palace chapel and felt very solemn. Today, before the Easter meal, Papa and Mama kissed all the servants and we helped hand out china eggs (fortunately Mama has a store of them).

Papa asked the officers who were on duty if they wanted to join us for the meal, and they did, but they didn't speak – in fact no one spoke much. Nothing felt the same. I couldn't even eat my usual enormous quantities of kulich and paskha. The best thing about the day was that Dr Botkin said I could go out for the first time – I haven't been out since before I had measles, which is more than a month ago. Before we're allowed to leave the palace, we have to meet in the round hall, and then a guard comes and unlocks the door. And then we can only go a little way into the park and we're followed everywhere by soldiers with bayonets – actually you feel more of a prisoner outside than in. We also have to return to the palace all together before the door is locked again.

Today Papa and Alexis worked at breaking the ice around the landing pier in the big lake and Olga, Tatiana and I walked a little. All the while you could see a crowd of people standing outside the park railings staring at us and sometimes calling out – you couldn't quite hear what, but you could tell it was rude. So now I know how it feels to be in a zoo. Despite all this it was awfully nice to be in the park again.

April 5th

Mama has a sentry posted right outside the window of her dressing room, so when she wants to get dressed she has to crouch behind a screen.

April 8th

We've all recovered now, even Marie, and I'm sorry to say it's been decided that lessons should start again. They're going to be shared out – Papa will teach history and geography, Mama religion, Countess Hendrikov English and art and Trina arithmetic. Monsieur Gilliard is going to be a kind of headmaster. It's a way of keeping us all busy, Papa says. I haven't mentioned Mr Gibbes because he's in Petrograd and they won't let him come back to us. He wrote a note to Alexis saying he would wait and hoped to return soon. As for Pyotr Vasilievich – he's gone, which I'm sorry about. He always seemed so fond of us, but maybe he felt embarrassed because of his son being a Menshevik and everything.

April 13th

Kerensky came to see us again. He talked to Papa first and then Mama. He's *still* asking her if she was secretly helping the Germans! The good news is that Papa and Mama don't have to be separated any more.

This afternoon we went into the park, for exercise. I threw sticks for Jimmy and Joy, and Papa and Alexis carried on with their ice-breaking. One of the people outside the railings shouted 'What are you going to do with yourself when the ice melts Citizen Romanov?' Papa didn't seem to hear.

April 18th

Marie and I both have Becker and stomach pains, so we're lying on our beds with hot water bottles. Jimmy is curled up beside me. Marie is writing to Grandmama and I'm writing this.

Something horrible happened yesterday. Monsieur Gilliard was going past Alexis's room when he heard Derevenko inside shouting things like 'Unlace my boots!' and 'Get a cushion for my head!' Monsieur Gilliard went in at once and found Derevenko lying on the sofa, ordering Alexis about like a *servant*. He went and told Papa and Derevenko left that afternoon. Nagorny is furious with him – he says that Derevenko had been spending too much time with the guards and it had turned his head – but still I can hardly believe he could do that when he's looked after Alexis for years and years. And we always liked him so.

Alexis doesn't seem terribly upset – I said, 'Didn't you mind being treated like that?' and he just shrugged and said, 'Well, at first I thought it was a game and then I didn't want to make him angry.' He says he minds people being rude to Papa much more. Alexis is really quite different these days, more grown-up and thoughtful I suppose, but also quieter and more serious. Sometimes I miss his naughtiness.

April 23rd

I got a letter from Aunt Olga today. She's in the Crimea, with Grandmama and Uncle Sandro and Aunt Xenia and our cousins. Felix and Irina are there too. She says that they live very quietly and, most of the time, they're left in peace, but occasionally they get a visit from revolutionary soldiers or some official from the new government (of course she's careful about what she writes because she knows our letters get read). She says they've had to make a good many economies, like sending away servants. When she described the blossom coming out everywhere I felt terribly homesick for Livadia. Please God may we be able to go there.

I've found out that Pyotr Vasilievich didn't abandon us after all – he went away from Tsarskoe Selo for a little holiday (before the revolution) and then he fell ill with pneumonia. He's still not better. I don't know if he'll be allowed to come back to us, but I'm going to write and tell him our news.

May 2nd

We've all had our heads shaved – our hair has been falling out since the measles and this should make it grow back properly. The funny thing is it makes us look nearly identical – well us girls at least. We wear scarves to hide our bald noodles when we go out!

May 6th

Sunday. Went to mass and confession. Alexis's arm is hurting him – he must have knocked it but he can't remember how – and he's in bed. I helped him with his model village this morning and now Mama and Tatiana are with him.

After lunch, I went for a walk with Olga, Marie and Papa and, just as we were heading towards the small lake, a soldier came in front of Papa, sort of pushed him with his shoulder and said, 'You can't go there, Mr Colonel.' Papa turned round at once and beckoned to us to follow him back to the palace. Olga got all red in the face and said she couldn't bear to hear Papa spoken to like that, but Papa didn't seem the least bit bothered and just said, 'Don't waste your anger on these ruffians.'

They really are ruffians – their uniforms are filthy and their hair and beards are all greasy and straggly. Did a puzzle after dinner, while Papa read us *The Count of Monte Cristo*.

May 11th

Marie and I had English – a dictation – with Countess Hendrikov this morning. She's not a very good teacher, not nearly as good as Mr Gibbes. She didn't even notice that I'd spelled mischievous 'mischeivous'. Then we had medieval history with Papa and we got in a fearful muddle with names and dates and Papa had to keep checking in his text book!

In the afternoon I went into the park with my sisters (Alexis still isn't well) and Monsieur Gilliard. We asked him to take a photograph of us, but first to shut his eyes for a minute. Then we all pulled off our head scarves and I said, 'Open your eyes Monsieur Gilliard and snap!' He looked really quite embarrassed and said that he didn't think he should take a picture of us like that – four baldies – but we made him. I can't wait to see it.

May 12th

A man called Colonel Kobylinsky has arrived to take command of the soldiers here. He looks friendly and he's very respectful towards Papa.

May 16th

We have a new interest – gardening! Colonel Kobylinsky has given us permission to plant a vegetable garden in front of the palace. We have to dig up the turf first, then make the beds and prepare the soil and sow seeds. Papa is going to direct operations, but it turns out Trina knows all about gardening, because her father had a market garden where she grew up, near Paris, so she'll be chief adviser.

May 18th

Ortino, Tatiana's bulldog, died yesterday. He was eleven. We buried him in the park, with a proper service.

May 23rd

Our garden is coming along famously. It's jolly hard work though, especially the digging. This afternoon, Papa, Olga, Tatiana, Alexis and I worked at it for nearly three hours (Marie is always trying to get out of digging – today she said she'd hurt her back). Monsieur Gilliard helped and Trina and some of the servants, and even a few soldiers joined in – they actually smiled at us and looked quite friendly.

We've planted potatoes, beetroot, lettuces, carrots, sorrel, radishes and 500 cabbages! We're going to have some flower beds too, underneath the palace windows – mostly roses. Mama was wheeled outside in her chair so she could watch us. The weather is beautifully warm.

May 25th

The servants are going to have their own garden, so Papa and all of us – even Marie! – went to help them dig the beds. Now they can grow whatever they like.

May 27th

We've planted roses in the beds under the windows and now we're digging some more flower beds in the orchard – they're going to be for wilder kinds of flowers, like poppies and daisies. I'd like to grow lily of the valley for Mama, but Trina says we don't have the right conditions.

It's funny, sometimes, and especially while we've been doing the garden, with everyone joining in and chatting and laughing, I quite forget about the revolution, or Papa abdicating, or us being prisoners. It's as if nothing's happened. In fact, if you ignore the guards, our life isn't so bad. There are lessons in the morning – and often they feel like playing at lessons because of our stand-in teachers – and afternoons in the park, and then cosy evenings with Papa reading to us, while we knit or embroider or do the albums. Also, I keep forgetting that the war's still going on, though of course Papa follows the news – he says our troops are making advances at the moment.

I do miss working in the hospital (I sometimes wonder where Andrei Vasilievich is now), but then I do love having Papa with us all the time and I think he feels the same. He said this afternoon, while we were working in the orchard, 'There's one great benefit in being an ex–Emperor – I get to spend every day with my family!' I talked about this with Tatiana and Marie and they feel like me, but I think Mama and Olga and Alexis mind more.

May 28th

Well, yesterday I was writing that I can sometimes forget that anything's happened and then something happens to remind you. When Papa and I and Alexis were coming in from the park this afternoon, Papa put out his hand to the officer standing in front of the door and he turned away. Papa said, 'My dear fellow, won't you even shake hands?' and he didn't reply. I felt like biffing the man and Alexis looked like he was going to explode. But Papa just sighed and shook his head, though I could tell he was upset.

I think Colonel Kobylinsky must have heard about this because, later on, he told Papa that it would be better if he didn't offer his hand to the officers. How utterly stupid it is. Sometimes I can't bear the way Papa accepts everything – I wish he'd stand up for himself, that he'd tell these swine what he thinks of them. But of course I know it wouldn't do any good.

June 7th

The weather is sweltering now. Trina is a terrible stickler for watering. She insists that we give our vegetables a good soaking every day, which means dragging the water butt all the way from the stables. Trina is quite a different person in the garden. Usually she's quite timid and hardly ever offers an opinion about anything, but she has all sorts of opinions about gardening. Papa came bicycling with us girls, and Alexis and Nagorny rowed to the children's island in the big lake, where Alexis swam. Since the days are so long now we're allowed to stay out until eight.

June 10th

Alexis has found a new way to keep us entertained – he puts on film shows in his room with a projector and films that he was given by the Pathé film company (before the revolution). He takes it very seriously. We have to line up and buy tickets and sit in rows, and then Alexis comes to the front of the room and makes a little bow and announces the programme! Unfortunately the programme doesn't change much because he only has six films.

Lenka – he's our footman – brought us some wild raspberries today. Lenka's parents used to be servants here – his mother was Olga's nursemaid and his father was a groom – but they're both dead now, so in a way we've become his family. He's only fourteen.

June 11th

Marie and I were in our room last night when we heard a shot outside, very close. A few minutes later Papa came in with one of the officers, who said that a sentry had fired because he thought someone was signalling with a red lamp from our window. So I explained that I'd been sitting in the window, sewing, and using the lamp, which has a red shade, and the officer realised that when I moved in front of the light it must have looked like signalling. I said, 'Well I'm glad you didn't blow my head off!' but nobody laughed. This morning we actually found a bullet in the window frame, so it really *was* lucky I didn't get my head blown off.

June 18th

My sixteenth birthday! I used to look forward to being sixteen – to getting my first diamonds from Papa and Mama and perhaps having a ball like the one Olga had at Livadia. Well, there are certainly no diamonds and no ball. In fact I was surprised to get any presents at all – Papa gave me a book on horticulture and Mama a collar that she'd embroidered. My sisters gave me a bottle of my favourite Coty Violette perfume (I don't know where they got that from). And I got an 'interesting' (his word) rock from Alexis.

Count Benckendorff arranged to have some champagne for dinner, so everyone drank my health and then Olga played the piano. It wasn't the birthday I'd always imagined, but I keep telling myself that the important thing is that we're all together and we won't live like this for ever. We can't. I'm sure my next birthday will be quite different.

June 20th

Yesterday Alexis was playing near the lake with his toy rifle (it has wooden bullets and it once belonged to our grandpapa), when an officer came up and said that some of the soldiers had demanded that he 'give up his weapon'. Alexis started to cry and ran to Mama, who was sitting on a rug nearby, and she and Monsieur Gilliard tried to explain that it was just a toy, not a weapon, but the officer insisted and took it away. Then, in the evening, when we were sitting down to dinner, Colonel Kobylinsky came in and apologised and said that of course Alexis could have the gun back, but so as not to anger the soldiers he's taken it apart and he's returning it to Alexis piece by piece, hidden under his coat. Alexis has been told he can only play with it in his room.

Lenka helped me water the garden. Papa has started reading us *A Study in Scarlet* by Arthur Conan Doyle. It's a detective story and terrifically exciting – we beg him not to stop.

June 25th

We sampled our first radishes and lettuces today – delicious! The carrots and sorrel are nearly ready too. Tatiana and I weeded all afternoon. As were doing the last bed, Tatiana suddenly said, 'You're not nearly as aggravating as you used to be, Anastasia – you've grown up at last.' Which is her idea of a compliment. So I said, 'Well, as it happens, you're a lot less aggravating too.' And when I thought about it I realised it's true – she's still bossy, but she's not so superior and convinced she's always right.

Papa, Prince Dolgorukov and Monsieur Gilliard have started cutting down and sawing up trees in the park – it'll be firewood for winter and Papa likes the exercise. Our troops have had lots of victories over the Germans lately, so Papa has ordered a Te Deum to give thanks.

July 6th

It seems the war isn't going so well now and Papa is worried. And there has also been some kind of trouble in Petrograd. Shura told me this evening that she'd heard from her brother – he lives in Petrograd – that people are starving and they've been marching in the streets and protesting against the war and the government. It's been absolutely pouring with rain and now it's much cooler.

July 12th

Kerensky came to see Papa yesterday and they were shut away for ages in Papa's study. Kerensky is now Prime Minister of the Provisional Government. Papa says he's come to think that he's really a good fellow and that we can definitely trust him to look after us. At dinner Papa told us that because of the trouble in Petrograd we might be sent away from Tsarskoe Selo. I said, 'Will we go to Livadia?' and Papa said, 'Very possibly'.

We've been told to start packing, but secretly, so the guards don't notice – it's better that they shouldn't realise that we're leaving. We're all awfully excited – even Mama looks cheery and is busy giving the maids instructions about pressing her muslin dresses and steaming hats. I think we could live very happily at Livadia. Marie and I stayed awake for hours talking about it.

July 22nd

We had another visit from Kerensky. I dug some of our potatoes – still quite small, but big enough to eat. Papa chopped wood, and then he and Marie and I rowed on the lake while Alexis swam around the children's island and did his best to splash us.

July 28th

Bad news – we're not being sent to the Crimea. Count Benckendorff told us after lunch today that we're going to some town in the east, and that we should pack warm clothes. We leave soon. It is a great disappointment not to be going to Livadia, but I think I'm glad to be going *somewhere*. Papa and Mama have had to decide who will come with us. I think it's going to be Prince Dolgorukov, Countess Hendrikov, Dr Botkin, Monsieur Gilliard and Trina. Count Benckendorff has to stay behind because his wife is very ill. Of course lots of the servants will come too.

Mama says we're to take all our jewels (I hardly have any, but Mama and the others do). I suppose we might not come back to Tsarskoe Selo. Everyone is restless and rather nervous.

July 30th

Today is Alexis's birthday – he's thirteen – and tomorrow we're leaving! To celebrate Alexis's birthday, our favourite icon at Znamenia was brought from the church in a procession across the park all the way to the palace chapel, where we had the service. When Father Vasilev started saying prayers for our safe journey, I looked around the chapel and noticed that nearly everyone was in tears – Mama, Olga, Marie, Count Benckendorff, Countess Hendrikov, even Colonel Kobylinsky. It suddenly felt rather frightening – I hadn't really thought before that we might not be safe. We kissed the icon (so did some of the soldiers, which was quite surprising) and then it was carried away back across the park as we all stood on the terrace and watched.

July 31st

I'm writing this sitting in the round hall surrounded by all our luggage. The soldiers refused to carry it until Count Benckendorff agreed to pay them three roubles each. It's nearly eleven o'clock at night and Alexis is running around like a mad thing, as are Jimmy and Joy, while the rest of us are rather quiet and apprehensive. We're waiting to leave, but nobody seems to know exactly when that's going to be.

Most of today was spent saying goodbyes. Marie and Alexis and I walked around the park and said goodbye to all our favourite places – the children's island, the best tobogganing bank, the tree we carved our initials on, Alexis's donkey Vanka and our garden (it's bursting with vegetables which we'll never get to eat, but Papa has arranged for the servants who're staying here to have them). Then we had to say goodbye to the servants who aren't coming with us, like Shura, which made me awfully sad because I've known Shura practically my whole life and, even though she says she'll come and find me when we've settled into our new home, I know I might not see her again. Also Count Benckendorff – he's very old so I'm sure we won't see him. He said, 'God bless you, Anastasia Nicolaevna – make sure you keep everyone's spirits up,' in a very shaky voice. About half an hour ago, who should appear but Uncle Misha. Kerensky has given him permission to say goodbye to Papa and now they're in Papa's study.

Midnight – we're still waiting. Uncle Misha didn't stay long with Papa – he came out of the study and gave us all a quick kiss and then he was gone. He had tears in his eyes. Papa says it was impossible to say a proper goodbye because Kerensky stayed in the room with them, which made things awkward. Not long ago I saw Papa go up to the table, where the officers are sitting drinking tea, and ask for a glass. One of the officers said, 'Don't expect me to sit at the same table as Nicholas Romanov!' and Papa shrugged and turned away. I went to give him a hug because I hate it when people are so rude. Now Papa's just told me that the officer came and apologised and explained that he only said what he did because he's afraid that the soldiers will accuse him of being a counter-revolutionary – that means you're against the revolution.

2 a.m. – Half an hour ago we were told to put on our coats and go out to the terrace, but it was a false alarm. There's some problem with the train and Kerensky has gone to telephone the station again. Alexis is still wandering about and annoying everyone by asking questions. Mama, Tatiana and Marie are trying to rest on the drawing room sofas. Olga is reading – how can she? Papa is talking to Colonel Kobylinsky. And Countess Hendrikov and Trina are playing patience and drinking tea.

August 3rd, on the train
Well we finally left Tsarskoe Selo at about six in the morning, just as the sun was rising. Now we're on a train – it's not like our own train, but it isn't too bad. When we stop at stations we have to keep the blinds pulled down so no one can see us. We're going to Tobolsk, which is a town in Siberia. Kerensky told Papa that it's a safe place and we

won't have to be there for very long, just until things settle down.

We're keeping quite cheerful. Dr Botkin has brought his children, Gleb and Tatiana, with him, so we play with them. And we play cards for hours with Trina and Monsieur Gilliard, and games like 'I packed my trunk with…' The worst thing is it's terribly hot and we absolutely swelter in our carriage. Colonel Kobylinsky has come with us and also General Tatischev – he was with Papa at Stavka and he's Count Benckendorff's replacement. We have breakfast at eight, lunch at one, tea at five and dinner at eight, but the food isn't very nice. And the train stops every evening so we can get out for some exercise and walk the dogs. Mama isn't well – all the upheaval has strained her heart, so she stays on the train.

A funny thing happened yesterday – the train stopped, out in the country, and I peeped out of the window and saw a little boy who came up and said, 'Uncle, do you have a newspaper you could give me?' So I said, 'I'm an auntie, not an uncle and I don't have a newspaper.' At first I couldn't think what he meant about being an uncle, and then I remembered that I wasn't wearing my scarf and my hair is still as short as a boy's! Some of the soldiers were standing near when this happened and we all laughed a lot. Tomorrow night we'll be in Tiumen and from there we're going to continue our journey by boat.

August 5th, on the Russia

Now we're on a steamboat called the *Russia*, which will

take us all the way to Tobolsk. Papa, Mama and Alexis have one cabin and we girls another. We've got bunk beds. Tatiana snored last night and then she was furious when I told everyone – she's not the kind of person who likes to admit she snores. We were quite amazed this morning when we sailed past Pokrovskoe, which is the village that Our Friend came from, and we could actually see his house (it's much bigger than the other houses) and people standing on the balcony. Mama says that Our Friend had predicted that one day she would visit his village and he was right! But I don't know if he predicted that we'd visit it like this, as prisoners. Sometimes I think that it would be a comfort, especially for Mama, if Our Friend was still alive.

August 7th

We arrived in Tobolsk yesterday evening. From the deck we could see the outline of church domes, and some kind of fortress, for ages before we actually docked. Colonel Kobylinsky and Prince Dolgorukov went ashore to inspect the Governor's house, which is where we're going to live. But when they came back they said that the house was in a dreadful state – dirty and with no furniture – and that it wasn't possible to move in. So now we have to stay on the *Russia* until it's ready for us.

August 10th

We're still living on the *Russia*. I must say it's not much fun – it's awfully cramped and our cabin is absolutely tiny and there's nowhere to wash properly. I think I'm going to get Becker soon and I really don't want to still be here then. Jimmy keeps doing the Governor on deck and I have to clear up after him. In the afternoons we steam along the river for a bit and then stop and take a walk along the bank. So that's something. But otherwise there's nothing to do. Mama is feeling bad and Alexis's arm is hurting him – Monsieur Gilliard spends most of the day in his cabin trying to distract him. I've been quarrelling with Tatiana, for the first time in ages. The highlight of the day is when Papa reads us Sherlock Holmes after dinner.

August 15th

We've finally moved into our new home – well, I can't quite think of it as a home, but it's a place to live. Papa, Olga, Marie, Alexis and I walked here this morning along extremely dusty streets and Mama and Tatiana followed in a carriage. There were soldiers everywhere. The house is quite large and white. It's on 'Freedom Street', which is rather a joke. Our rooms are on the first floor – my sisters and I are going to share a corner room, Papa and Mama have another and Alexis has his own (Nagorny will sleep next door to him). The dining room and drawing room are downstairs and Monsieur Gilliard will have a little room next to the drawing room. Even though the Governor's house is meant to be the biggest in Tobolsk it still feels tiny compared to the Alexander Palace!

At twelve o'clock we had mass and a priest sprinkled our rooms with holy water, and then we had lunch in the dining room with the suite, or at least what's left of it – Prince Dolgorukov, General Tatischev, Countess Hendrikov, Dr Botkin and Trina. Afterwards we went to inspect their house. It's across the street from us and it's called the Kornilov house because it's owned by a merchant called Kornilov. It all feels very strange and not at all nice, but Mama says that once we've unpacked and arranged all the things we brought with us from Tsarskoe Selo it'll seem much more homely.

August 18th

We're trying to settle in. Our carpets and pictures and lamps and things have been put around our rooms. There are lots of photographs in the drawing room and we've installed the gramophone too. I've put up my icons and photographs above my bed and arranged my glass bottles and combs and things on the little bedside table (our beds are close together and there's not much space). And Tatiana has put lots of cushions on the sofa in our room and some lace hangings on the walls. It does feel better.

August 19th

For the first couple of days here we were allowed to cross the street to visit the Kornilov house, but the soldiers objected, so now that's been stopped and they're building a big wooden fence around our house. Our people can come and go between our house and theirs, and go for walks and things, but we can only take exercise inside the fence.

When I remember the park at Tsarskoe Selo I feel horribly homesick – I know we were prisoners there, but it was quite easy to forget that. Here, you can't forget for a minute. Sometimes, like now, I feel furious about everything – why are we being punished like this? It's so unfair! And why does no one help us? What about all the people who supported Papa, and the President of France who was always giving us presents, and the King of England who was supposed to be so fond of us? Why don't they do anything? I sometimes even feel angry with Papa – I often think about all the things Sovanna and Andrei Vasilievich used to say about how Russia needed to change, and I wonder whether he couldn't have stopped the revolution.

August 20th

I feel terrible for writing that about Papa – I know there's no one as good and no one who loves Russia more.

August 24th

The weather is hot and beautiful, and it's extremely frustrating that we can only walk up and down our dusty yard. Papa minds especially and it's miserable for Jimmy and Joy. Because we aren't allowed to go to church, we have services in the hall – we've made a kind of altar (Mama's bedspread has become the altar cloth) and put up icons and lamps. The local priest, Father Alexei, comes to lead the prayers. He's got a very kind face and it feels like he'll be a friend to us. Four nuns came with him for this morning's service – they sang beautifully and we all felt much better afterwards.

August 28th

Some telegrams arrived today with news of the war. Not good news – our troops are retreating. Papa is depressed about this. He said at lunch, 'I believed my abdication would help Russia win the war and now the government and the generals are simply making a mess of things.' He longs for proper news, but since letters take ages to get to us and newspapers are at least a week out of date – that's if we can get hold of one – it's jolly difficult.

August 29th

I think the people of Tobolsk feel quite friendly towards us. When I went onto the balcony this afternoon, with Mama and Tatiana, people looked up and bowed to us and, even when they're just walking past our house, you can see them taking off their hats and crossing themselves.

Presents of food keep arriving too – the nuns at the convent send us sugar and cakes and we get butter and eggs from local farmers nearly every day. So it doesn't look like I'm going to get thin!

September 1st

Two commissars from the Provisional Government have arrived to take charge of us (Colonel Kobylinsky is staying, which we're all relieved about, but he'll just be in command of the guards). The new commissars are called

Vasily Pankratov – he's the head – and Alexander Nikolsky – he's the deputy. They're living in the Kornilov house. They came to introduce themselves to us after lunch today. Vasily Pankratov is small with bushy hair and eyebrows and very thick spectacles – he looks like a professor. Papa was very polite to him and he was very respectful towards Papa and asked if we needed anything. Papa told him about the plumbing, which is dreadful – the downstairs W.C. keeps overflowing, the pipes are blocked and we've had to stop having baths – and he promised to get it fixed at once. Papa also asked if he could arrange for him to chop wood in the yard and he said he would.

While Pankratov was talking to us Nikolsky stood behind him and stared at us in a very sneering kind of way and didn't take off his cap. He's quite tall and he's got a wide, flat, pink face and piggy eyes. I don't like him.

September 4th

We have to have our photographs taken for identity cards. Apparently it's Nikolsky's idea and he insists, even though Colonel Kobylinsky said it was quite unnecessary since everyone knows exactly who we are.

September 5th

We – that's our family and the suite – lined up yesterday to be photographed by a man from Tobolsk. Alexis got into trouble with Nikolsky because he went to stand by the photographer, to watch what he was doing. Nikolsky shouted, 'Get out of the way, boy, and go back upstairs!' Alexis looked quite amazed – I don't think anyone has ever called him 'boy' before! Now we have cards with our photograph, name and number and we're supposed to keep them with us.

September 8th

Commissar Pankratov has arranged for us to go to mass on Sunday mornings at the local church. We went for the first time today. To get there we had to walk through the town park, past rows of soldiers lined up on each side of the path. Do they really think we're going to try and run away? Still, it was a great comfort to be in a proper church – Mama cried, out of thankfulness.

September 17th

Some crates of wine arrived from Tsarskoe Selo a couple of days ago. Some of the soldiers, and Nikolsky of course, don't think we should be allowed to have them, so it's been decided the bottles should be thrown into the river. We watched from the balcony as the crates were loaded onto a cart and driven off, with Nikolsky sitting on top of them, holding an axe.

September 26th

Well, we've been here for over a month now and I can't say it feels like home, but we have settled into a kind of routine. Lessons begin at nine – that's for Marie, me and Alexis. We have them in the hall or in Monsieur Gilliard's room (it's a great bore to be still having lessons, but it does pass the time). While we're improving our minds (ha!) Mama, Olga and Tatiana generally sew – our clothes are getting very worn and need mending all the time and Alexis is growing out of his. At eleven we go out into the yard for a walk with Papa. Luncheon is at one and then, in the afternoon, we go out again. There are some tree trunks in the yard now and we all take it in turns to saw and chop them up into logs for the kitchen and the stoves. It may not be a particularly ladylike pastime, but I've actually grown very fond of wood-chopping! And it gives us some exercise. We have competitions – who can chop the most logs in ten minutes. Tatiana and Papa usually win. Marie, naturally, is a hopeless slow-coach.

Tatiana and Gleb Botkin quite often join us. Alexis likes playing with Gleb, but Tatiana is only ten, so she's rather too young. Then we have tea at four and afterwards we read, or write letters, or play music. That's when I write this. Dinner's at eight. After dinner we girls sew and Alexis does a puzzle or makes his models, while Papa reads aloud. Mama likes playing bezique with General Tatischev. You could almost say it's cosy.

September 30th

We got very excited yesterday because Dr Botkin received a note from Kerensky, which said that we could go for walks outside the town. But when Papa asked Pankratov when that could start, he just said it was out of the question because it wasn't safe. It's a great disappointment.

We all long for a sight of the country, and trees

especially. I often sit with Marie looking out of the window of our room at the people passing by, and notice little things about them, or imagine what their lives are, but it's still a pretty boring view. These days I think I really wouldn't mind if we never had any money again, or servants, or palaces, or new clothes or anything. I'd be quite happy if we could just live in the Crimea, not even at Livadia, just in a little house, and perhaps Papa could be a farmer, like he's often said he'd like to be. As long as we were free.

October 6th

I'm sitting in the hall, where we usually have tea. It's always dark in here because of the fence. Alexis is playing with his soldiers at the table, Olga and Papa are reading, Tatiana is writing a letter and Marie is playing patience. Mama is lying down as her heart is troubling her. She had lunch upstairs, with Alexis, in Papa's study – she often does that. I keep having to go out into the yard to chase Jimmy and Joy, who never stop trying to steal bits of food from the rubbish dump. Jimmy is getting very fat in consequence. They need proper walks, poor things. Mr Gibbes has arrived in Tobolsk, but we haven't seen him yet.

October 7th

It felt cold today for the first time. Siberian winters are famously cold, so we're bracing ourselves to freeze. Mr Gibbes was allowed to come and see us this morning. He's not the kind of man who shows his feelings much, but I think he was pleased to see us, and we were certainly delighted to see him. We bombarded him with questions about Petrograd. He says there are lots of disturbances and protests against the government and the streets are filthy.

After we left Tsarskoe Selo he was allowed to go there to collect his things and then he tried to set off for Tobolsk, but a railway strike delayed him and then the journey took nearly two weeks and there was nowhere to wash on the train so he kept having to jump into freezing rivers to get clean! (Mr Gibbes is a great stickler for cleanliness.) Anyway, he got here. He's going to move into the Kornilov house and he'll start lessons tomorrow. Now he's having a talk with Papa.

October 10th

We took communion in the church this morning, which was wonderful. Then I had English composition with Mr Gibbes. I had to turn a poem, by an English poet called Tennyson, into prose, which was not at all easy. I said, 'Don't you think my English has greatly improved, Mr Gibbes?' (it hasn't). He looked at me carefully and replied, in his precise way, 'I sincerely hope that's the case, Anastasia Nicolaevna, but it's rather too early to ascertain.' I said, 'I can see you've missed me, Mr Gibbes!' And he blushed!

Afterwards, Trina took me aside and said that maybe it wasn't altogether fair to flirt with Mr Gibbes. As if I was! I told her not to be ridiculous and couldn't she tell the difference between flirting and teasing and anyway we've *always* teased Mr Gibbes. She said, 'Well, you're not a child any more, Anastasia, and perhaps Mr Gibbes *can't* tell the difference.' Honestly. Does being grown-up just mean you have to be careful all the time? Jimmy has eaten something bad from the rubbish and made himself sick.

October 22nd

We've actually made friends with a good many of the soldiers, especially the ones from the 4th Regiment (the men from the 2nd Regiment aren't so friendly). We chat to them in the yard and sometimes even in the guardhouse and Marie and I are trying to learn the names of all their wives and children – we test each other. The more you talk to them, the more you realise they're really just like the men who used to be in our hospital. I don't think they want to be guarding us much – they'd prefer to be home with their families. Papa agrees with me. He and Alexis sometimes go into the guardhouse to play draughts with some of the men from the 4th Regiment, and they give Alexis old nails and stones for his collections.

I wrote a letter to Pyotr Vasilievich after tea – I've asked him if he could send me the set of Tolstoy books that Papa gave me. I left them in the schoolroom bookcase at Tsarskoe Selo. I don't suppose he'll be able to. My hair is long enough now not to have to wear a scarf any more.

October 27th

Papa and Prince Dolgorukov have put up some swings in

the yard – that may not sound like much, but it's a great excitement here!

October 30th

The Engineer-mechanic* arrived this morning and I've got bad cramps, so I'm spending the day in bed with a hot water bottle. It's been snowing for the last two days. When we first came here we noticed that somebody had scratched 'Anna darling' on the glass of our bedroom window. I keep looking at it and wondering who wrote it and who Anna was and what's become of her.

November 1st

Had French this morning with Trina. She hasn't had a letter from her father since she's been here and she's worried about him. I told her that all letters seem to take weeks and weeks to get to us, and some probably don't get here at all. Mama isn't well, so she had lunch upstairs with Alexis. She looks really quite old these days. I know God is a great consolation to her, well her only consolation really. She often says, 'Be strong, my girlies – God won't abandon us,' but it doesn't always seem enough. Anyway, it feels to me as though God *has* abandoned us.

November 2nd

Papa has heard news from Petrograd – there's been another revolution! The Provisional Government has fallen and the Bolsheviks have taken control. I'm not absolutely sure who the Bolsheviks are – Papa just says they're scoundrels and they'll bring Russia to her knees. I know they don't believe Russia should have a tsar. Kerensky has fled and now someone called Lenin is in charge. We can only get the local newspaper, which doesn't tell you much, but Papa simply falls on it and reads every word.

A parcel arrived from Ania today with some clothes – dresses and stockings – for my sisters and me. We certainly need them. Ania was put into prison after she was taken away from Tsarskoe Selo and she spent five whole months there. Now she's living with her parents in Petrograd. She says she's still very lame. Mama writes to her a lot.

November 12th

Mr Gibbes gave Marie and me a dictation this morning, from Mr Oscar Wilde. I kept asking Mr Gibbes to repeat himself and eventually he became quite cross and said, 'Will you shut up and listen, Anastasia Nicolaevna!' So now I've written my name on the front of my exercise books as 'Anastastia Nicolaevna Shut-up'. I know I mustn't torment Mr Gibbes, but it's so easy that sometimes I just can't resist and, after all, what else is there to do?

Marie and I have made particular friends with two soldiers (from the 4th Regiment). They're called Ivan Ivanovich and Igor Leontich. Ivan is quite fat – he likes to rest his hands on his belly when he talks to you. He's 31 and he's got a wife and five children, who don't live very far from Tobolsk, but he never gets to see them. He used to be a carpenter. Igor is very skinny. He's 25 and he's engaged to be married – his sweetheart lives in a village in the Urals. He's very fond of dogs so Jimmy is a great favourite with him.

There's quite a lot of snow now – we've been swinging high on the swings and then jumping off into it – but still not enough to build a snow mountain. Mama doesn't come out any more as the cold is too much for her heart.

November 19th

Papa is very upset because the Bolsheviks have signed an armistice with the Germans.

November 26th

Papa got a letter from Grandmama and he read out parts of it at tea. She says they feel quite cut off at Ai-Todor as they're not allowed to leave and no one is allowed in to see them apart from Irina. Grandmama has lunch every day with Aunt Xenia and Aunt Olga and our cousins. They feel hungry a lot of the time because it's hard to get provisions and she especially misses white bread and butter. She says their guards are mostly polite and friendly. The most exciting news is that Aunt Olga has had a baby! It's a boy and she'd wanted to have a baby for ages so we're all very happy for her. This evening we played a very noisy game of hide and seek around the house with Gleb and Tatiana Botkin.

November 30th

I'm writing this in the drawing room after dinner. We're

drinking tea and hot chocolate. Mama is knitting stockings for Alexis and I've been trying to knit a hat for Aunt Olga's baby but, since it's proving awfully difficult and Papa has started to read us *The Three Musketeers*, I've given up!

December 6th

We're beginning to understand what a Siberian winter means. Outside it's 28 degrees below zero and inside it's not a lot warmer – about 44 degrees. And our bedroom, because it's on the corner, is an absolute ice-box. We huddle around the stoves and never take our capes and coats off. Mama and Tatiana have chilblains. We've started making Christmas presents – ribbon bookmarks, and knitted stockings and waistcoats.

December 13th

Monsieur Gilliard and Mr Gibbes are going to help us put on some little plays. The idea is that it'll pass the time and maybe cheer everyone up a bit. We're going to start with *The Bear* by Chekhov and Papa is to take the lead part, of Smirnov. We're trying to persuade Dr Botkin to take the part of the doctor, but he keeps saying he has his professional dignity to think of. I said, 'What professional dignity is that, Dr Botkin?' I think he'll give in. Trina is going to be set and costume designer and Nyuta, Mama's maid, is going to do make-up.

December 16th

We rehearse every day after tea. Monsieur Gilliard and Mr Gibbes can never agree about stage directions. Dr Botkin *has* given in.

December 19th

The Bear had its opening night yesterday. We had programmes, written out by Mama, and the drawing room became a theatre, with the help of a curtain rigged up by Trina. The audience, which consisted of Mama, Countess Hendrikov, Prince Dolgorukov, General Tatischev, Trina, Tatiana and the servants were most enthusiastic and applauded wildly. Marie forgot her lines twice and had to be prompted by Mr Gibbes. We're already planning our next theatrical.

December 24th

Christmas Eve. This morning we helped Mama get everyone's presents ready, and then at teatime we went to the guardhouse with Mama and Papa and prepared a tree for the 4th Regiment. Mama gave each of the soldiers a Gospel and one of her bookmarks. Later on we did a tree for the suite and then we did ours. I got a pair of woollen stockings, a scarf (embroidered by Mama) and some chocolate. After dinner there was a service, in the hall, with quite a big choir of nuns. Some of the soldiers came too. I know Mama did everything she could to make it a Christmassy Christmas, but it just wasn't.

December 27th

On Christmas morning we went to mass in the church and Father Alexei said the prayer for the long life and health of the Romanovs, which he's not meant to do since Papa abdicated. And now some of the soldiers from the 2nd Regiment, and Nikolsky I expect, have made a fuss and we're no longer allowed to go to church and will have to make do with services in the house, with a soldier present. Mama minds dreadfully about this.

1918

January 2nd

Olga, Tatiana and Alexis have German measles – they're in bed but fortunately they don't feel too bad. The 2nd Regiment, who aren't at all friendly to us, have elected a Soldiers' Committee.

January 3rd

The Soldiers' Committee have voted that no officer can wear epaulets on the shoulders of his uniform – and that means Papa too. Papa has colonel's epaulets, which were given to him by Grandpapa, and he says that he'll refuse to remove them. He's very proud of them. Ivan Ivanovich doesn't agree with the Soldiers' Committee at all and nor, he says, do any of the soldiers of the 4th Regiment. I think it's absolutely swinish.

January 5th

Marie is covered in spots now, but the others are already up. I suppose it'll be my turn next. Colonel Kobylinsky tried to tell the Soldiers' Committee that they can't force Papa to remove his epaulets, but they wouldn't listen. Then, after dinner, Prince Dolgorukov and General Tatischev came to find Papa in the drawing room and begged him to do as the Committee says, because otherwise the 2nd Regiment will only get angrier and make things more difficult for us all. Papa gave Mama a look and they went off and whispered in the corner for a moment and then Papa said that he'd agree.

We've started to build a snow mountain in the yard. Some of the soldiers – our friends from the 4th Regiment – are helping us. It's very, very cold – 30 below – but bright and sunny too.

January 8th

The snow mountain is looking splendid. We spent the afternoon watering it – to make it really icy – which means lugging buckets of water from the kitchen. Monsieur Gilliard, Lenka, Ivan Ivanovich and Igor Leontich all helped. It's so cold that unless you run, the water freezes on the way from the kitchen to the mountain. Papa still secretly wears his epaulets in our rooms – he just hides them under his coat when he goes out.

January 14th

I've got spots, which means German measles, I'm afraid.

January 18th

I only had to spend three days in bed and now I'm up and feeling quite recovered and longing to try out the snow mountain. Tatiana told me – she'd heard from Mama –that Colonel Kobylinsky tried to resign, because he doesn't feel he has proper authority over the guards any more, but Papa persuaded him not to abandon us.

This evening there's going to be a little play – 'In and Out of a Punt'. It has just two actors – Mr Gibbes and Tatiana. Mr Gibbes is taking it very seriously, which only makes Tatiana the more worried that she'll have a fit of giggles. Jimmy also has a starring role as the dog!

January 19th

The play went off beautifully. No giggling. Tatiana, Marie, Alexis and I had a wonderful time tobogganing down our mountain. We kept landing in a heap on top of each other at the bottom. Then Monsieur Gilliard had a go and ended up sitting on top of Tatiana's head and twisting his ankle, so now he's limping. It's too cold to have tea in the hall now, so we've taken to using Papa's study.

January 25th

It's Tatiana's birthday today – there was a Te Deum for her in the hall.

January 26th

This morning we were told that Pankratov and Nikolsky are to be sent away and we're to get new Bolshevik commissars from Moscow. I think Papa's worried about this – he says 'better the devil you know'. We certainly won't miss Nikolsky, but Pankratov wasn't so bad. Even worse though is that the soldiers from the 4th Regiment are also going. That means our friends. It's hard not to feel that everyone's deserting us.

January 28th

Ivan Ivanovich and Igor Leontich came to say goodbye to us all (they had to make sure no one from the Soldiers' Committee noticed). I asked them where they were being sent to, but they didn't know. Perhaps they'll be allowed to go home. When I was shaking hands with Igor he pressed a little packet into my hand, which turned out to be a wooden bird that he'd carved. It's hard not to cry when people are kind.

February 7th

We performed another play last night. It was called *Packing Up*, by Harry Grattan, and I had the main part, which happened to be a man. Near the end I had to turn my back to the audience, open my dressing gown and say, 'But I've packed my trousers, I can't go!' When I did this there was suddenly a lot of laughing and looking down I realised my dressing gown had got caught up, giving everyone a perfect view of my sadly large bottom in Papa's underwear! I went quite purple with embarrassment. Mama was actually crying with laughter – she said, 'Oh, Anastasia, I can't remember when I last laughed like that,' so I suppose that's something to be thankful for. It's typical that it should happen to me though (it never would to Tatiana). Anyway, due to popular demand, *Packing Up* is to have another performance tomorrow, *not* featuring my behind!

February 12th

Our snow mountain is being destroyed. A few days ago we stood on top of it to wave goodbye to the 4th Regiment. The next thing we knew, the Soldiers' Committee had decided that the mountain was dangerous, because we could be seen from the street. From the window of our room I can see soldiers demolishing it with pick-axes. This has made us all feel very depressed, especially Alexis.

I do wonder sometimes if we'll ever be rescued. Mama says there are lots of people who still support Papa – I think she gets letters from them. Apparently they're trying to help us, so we have to be prepared. Papa has started reading us *Ivanhoe*.

February 15th

Well, there seems to be nothing but bad news at the moment. This morning Colonel Kobylinsky told us that the government has decided that we're to be put on soldier's rations and that each of us will get just 600 roubles a month (and that's to come from our own money). It's not nearly enough to pay for all the servants or for all our food, so at lunch Papa said, 'Since everyone else seems to be appointing committees, I'm going to appoint one myself.' He's put General Tatishchev, Prince Dolgorukov and Monsieur Gilliard in charge of our household and expenses.

February 16th

Papa's 'committee' had its first meeting today. It's been decided that ten servants will have to be dismissed, which Papa and Mama feel very badly about as they've been so loyal to us. Also we'll no longer have butter or coffee. I'm trying to console myself that less food will mean less of me. I hate being so chubby and it's made worse because I'm short. It seems most unfair too – I don't eat any more than Olga or Tatiana and they're both very thin. Even Marie, who you could say is plump, is miles thinner than me.

February 20th

The soldiers who guard us now couldn't be more different from our friends in the 4th Regiment. They've got horrible scowling expressions and they look at us as if they really hate us. They carved rude words into the seats of our swings – Alexis noticed, but, before the rest of us could see, Papa removed the seats.

February 23rd

Our new regime means boring meals, but we're not actually hungry. Generally we have soup and meat or fish for lunch and meat with vegetables, or sometimes macaroni, for dinner. And the people in Tobolsk, who've heard about our rations, continue to send us presents of butter, coffee, cakes and jam.

Papa has built a kind of wooden platform on the roof of the greenhouse in the yard – it's not very high, but it means that on sunny days we can sit out and almost have a view. Alexis and I played our balalaikas this evening for the first time in ages.

February 27th

The last day of pancakes – Alexis ate sixteen at luncheon! All afternoon Papa sawed wood, my sisters and I chopped and Alexis stacked. The soldiers have now drawn rude pictures and words on the fence – horrible things about Mama and Our Friend and other things about us that I don't want to write. It's impossible not to notice. What I mind most is the idea of Papa seeing.

February 28th

Lent starts today, so Father Alexei came to conduct services this morning and this evening, and Mama and my sisters and I all sang.

March 4th

There's a carnival today and everyone is celebrating in Tobolsk. We can hear bells and mouth-organs and singing. We sat out on Papa's platform and smoked cigarettes and you could see the tops of sledges flying by. It makes you feel quite lonely – hearing sounds of people having fun.

March 6th

Russia has definitely made peace with Germany – the Bolsheviks have signed a treaty. Papa is very depressed – he says it's a terrible humiliation for Russia and he can't believe that Uncle Willy could do business with the Bolsheviks who are nothing but traitors. Prince Dolgorukov said he'd read in a newspaper that the Germans had asked that we should be handed over to them and Mama said, 'I would rather die in Russia than be saved by the Germans!' which I entirely agree with.

March 9th

It's getting warmer now and the snow is melting. Mama has started to sit on the balcony again – her heart has been better lately.

Last night, in our room, my sisters and I had a long talk about marriage. It started when Marie suddenly said, 'Do you think we'll ever get married?' So I said, 'What do you mean? Of course we will.' And she said, 'But what if we're never free? How will we find husbands then?' I hadn't really thought of that, because I don't believe we'll be prisoners for ever. Then Olga said she wouldn't mind being a spinster. I said, 'Don't you ever wish you'd accepted Prince Squinty Eyes of Rumania?' and we all collapsed laughing. Even Tatiana said she didn't mind if she got married or not and she'd be quite happy living at home and looking after Mama and Papa. And Tatiana is the sort of person who'd have hundreds of suitors. She'd be a good empress, or queen or something. Marie said, quite sadly,

'Well, I'd like a husband and six children.' And I'd like the same – that is, if anyone wanted to marry me, of course.

March 10th

After our conversation last night I suddenly had a terrific idea – Dr Botkin and Countess Hendrikov should get married. Dr Botkin would have a wife to look after him and Gleb and Tatiana would have a step-mother and Countess Hendrikov is getting pretty old now, so she's not likely to have many offers. I discussed it with Marie and she agreed about it being a terrific idea, so when Dr Botkin came to our room, to have a look at Marie's cold sore, I said, 'Have you ever considered re-marrying, Dr Botkin?' He replied, very firmly, 'I can assure you, Anastasia Nicolaevna, I have absolutely no intention of getting married again, so you can put any mischief right out of your head.' I still think it's a good idea, but he may need some convincing.

March 13th

The days drag terribly – there's nothing much to write because nothing much happens. We can't put on any more plays because of Lent, so there's not even that distraction. I've always thought that that sooner or later we'd be free, that we'd be sent away from Russia, or rescued. But now I'm not so sure. I'm afraid we've been forgotten. Olga, Tatiana and I chopped wood in the afternoon.

March 20th

We had borscht for lunch for the third day in a row. Kharitonov, our cook, does his best to make interesting meals, but it's almost impossible because he has so few ingredients.

March 22nd

Everyone seems jumpy and nervous. I think it's because a lot of Red Guards – they're Bolsheviks – have arrived in Tobolsk. Mama has been forbidden to sit on the balcony.

March 30th

Alexis has hurt himself. He was sliding down the stairs on a boat, with runners, that he used to use on the snow mountain, and he landed badly. Now he's got a haemorrhage in his groin and he's in a lot of pain. Poor Alexis, he's been so well for ages, but I must say tobogganing down the stairs was a jolly stupid thing to do.

Colonel Kobylinksy came to tell us that he's been ordered to move our people from the Kornilov house over to the Governor's house. Dr Botkin, Gleb and Tatiana are to be allowed to stay where they are, but the others will become prisoners like us. There's hardly any room in our house, so I'm not sure where everyone will sleep.

April 1st

Alexis is suffering terribly. Mama sits with him most of the time, though my sisters and I take turns as well. Monsieur Gilliard reads to him for hours. He can't eat and mostly he just lies crying and moaning. Yesterday I heard him say to Mama, 'I would like to die – I'm not afraid of death, but I'm so afraid of what they will do to us here.' At times like this I wish Our Friend was with us.

April 2nd

General Tatischev, Prince Dolgorukov, Countess Hendrikov and Mr Gibbes moved into our house today. It's a tight squeeze. We teased Mr Gibbes a lot because he refused to share a room with Monsieur Gilliard, so he's been put in a kind of shed, next to the kitchen. He also insisted on having his maid, Anfisa, with him. I said – I couldn't stop myself – 'Well, you and Anfisa will be very cosy in your little shed Mr Gibbes!' Of course we know he isn't attached to Anfisa, he's just very particular about his linen.

April 3rd

There was a search of our rooms this morning. Prince Dolgorukov's draughts set and Papa's dagger have been confiscated.

April 9th

A new commissar has arrived from Moscow. He's moved into the Kornilov house. My sisters and I think he might order another search, so after tea we burned all our letters and Marie and I are going to burn our diaries too – I think the rude things I've written about the guards could get us into trouble. Alexis is a little better. I sat with him and played cards.

April 10th

Well, I haven't burned my diary. Marie did, but I couldn't bear to. The new commissar came to see us this morning. He's called Vasili Vasilevich Yakovlev. He has very black hair and no beard and even though his clothes are like a worker's he sounds quite educated. He asked Papa if he was satisfied with our accommodation and the guards, and then he made a very quick inspection of the house and asked to see Alexis, who's still in bed. We all feel that Commissar Yakovlev is somehow going to make things worse for us.

April 12th

We were right. Commissar Yakovlev has come to take Papa away. After lunch he came to see Papa and Mama and told them that he'd been ordered take us all, but because Alexis is too ill to travel it'll just be Papa. He says that Papa will be quite safe and that anyone who wishes can go with him. They leave tonight. Papa asked Colonel Kobylinsky where he was being taken, but Colonel Kobylinsky wasn't sure – he thinks it might be Moscow.

After Yakovlev had left, Tatiana and I heard Mama crying in her room, so we went in and she told us what had happened and asked Tatiana to fetch Monsieur Gilliard. She kept saying that she didn't know what to do, that she felt she should be by Papa's side, but she couldn't bear to leave Alexis. Tatiana said, 'But Mama, there isn't much time – we have to make some kind of decision. I think Papa needs you with him.' Monsieur Gilliard agreed and said that, if Mama went with Papa, we would all take great care of Alexis, and after all he is getting better. That seemed to make up Mama's mind and she said, 'Yes, that's best. I'll go with the Tsar and trust Alexis to you.' Then she had to start getting ready.

Tatiana and I found Olga and Marie in our room and we had a sort of conference. We all felt that one of us should go with Papa and Mama. After arguing for a bit – of course Tatiana wanted to go – we decided on Marie. It was a process of elimination – Tatiana will be needed to take charge of the household here, Olga is the best person to look after Alexis, and I am considered too young, by Olga and Tatiana anyway, to be a help to Mama. Which leaves Marie. We announced this to Papa and Mama and they seemed to think it a good idea. Now everyone is rushing about, making preparations and packing.

April 13th

Yesterday was definitely the worst day of my life so far. Most of the evening was spent in Alexis's room. Mama had to explain to him that they were leaving, but that we would all follow in a few weeks' time. You could see he was trying to be brave, but every now and again he'd start to cry. Mama just sat by his bed holding his hand. She kept saying that she was praying for a thaw, because then it would be impossible to cross the rivers and their journey would have to be postponed.

At about 10 p.m. the suite joined us and we all drank tea. Then Papa and Mama went downstairs to say goodbye to the servants. Dr Botkin, Prince Dolgorukov, Nyuta and Lenka are going with Papa and Mama. Nyuta was in a dreadful state and kept crying and saying she didn't know what the Bolsheviks were going to do to her.

None of us could sleep. Then at four, just as it was getting light, the carriages arrived, well they were hardly carriages, just tarantasses*, with no seats or anything and only one with a roof. So the servants ran to get straw to put on the floors and a mattress for Mama to lie on. Mama asked Monsieur Gilliard to go back upstairs and stay with Alexis and then she said goodbye to each of us. When she embraced me she said, 'Now, Anastasia, I am relying on you to keep everyone cheerful.' We all cried and cried. Only Papa was calm. Commissar Yakovlev made Mama put on Dr Botkin's fur coat because he was worried she might be cold. Papa tried to join Mama and Marie in their tarantass, but Yakovlev said he had to travel separately, with him. Then they left. Olga, Tatiana and I went straight upstairs to our room. As we passed Alexis's door we could hear him sobbing. I have never felt less like cheering anyone up.

April 15th

No news of Papa, Mama and Marie. We try and fill our days as best we can – lessons have stopped for now and we spend most of the time with Alexis. He's better, but he still has a lot of pain in his leg. Monsieur Gilliard and Mr Gibbes read to him and we play cards – usually his favourite 'The slower you ride the farther you go '– or do puzzles.

Countess Hendrikov wants us to pray with her all the time – she's terrifically religious, even more than Mama I think – and when she's not praying she's painting religious pictures (I'm afraid to say they're not very good). She tried to distract us today by getting us to paint watercolours, but it's awfully hard to concentrate on anything. We played whist after dinner with her and Trina.

April 16th

We got a letter this morning, from Mama, that she'd written in Tiumen. They've had a terrible journey – when they crossed the river Irtysh the ice had melted so much that the water came right up to the horses' stomachs. At another river everyone had to get out and cross on foot. And then a wheel broke. The horses were changed five times, once in Pokrovskoe, Our Friend's village, where they actually stopped outside his house and saw his whole family looking at them out of the window. From Tiumen they're going to get a train, to Moscow probably. We all feel tremendously relieved, knowing they're safe.

April 19th

Alexis was awake and crying most of last night. Tatiana sat up with him, so now she's resting. I must admit I don't know what we'd do without Tatiana – she takes charge of everything. She talks to Kharitonov about meals and organises who will sit with Alexis and makes sure our clothes and linen are laundered and mended. Olga is very sensible, but Tatiana makes decisions. Sometimes bossiness can be a good thing! The weather feels quite warm now. In the afternoon Olga and I walked in the yard and played on the swings, but it wasn't much fun. I wrote a letter to Papa and Mama – I hope it reaches them.

April 20th

We heard from Papa and Mama again. They're not in Moscow after all, but Ekaterinburg, in the Urals. Why they're there we can't imagine – Papa's letter didn't explain, but as he knows his letters will be read he can't say very much. Tatiana asked Colonel Kobylinsky if he knew why they'd been taken to Ekaterinburg, but he didn't. Anyway, Papa says they're living in a house that belongs to a merchant called Ipatiev. It's quite clean and they have five big rooms. Every piece of their luggage was searched when they arrived. For some reason Prince Dolgorukov hasn't been allowed to join them. Papa writes: 'We don't know how it will be here.'

April 22nd

It was Easter yesterday. We'd decorated the iconostasis* with pine branches and flowers and it looked quite splendid. Father Alexei came and took the service, which was very comforting. Then we handed out the Easter eggs that Mama had left (we'd painted them), to the suite and the servants. The Easter meal was dismal – no one could be jolly, least of all me, and all we could think about was Papa and Mama and Marie. A couple of the soldiers wandered in and just cut themselves a slice of our kulich without asking. Jimmy has a cold.

April 25th

A note arrived written by Nyuta but obviously dictated by
Mama. It said 'dispose of the medicines as agreed'. We
know what that means. It's code. We have to start hiding
our jewels by sewing them into our clothes.

April 27th

'Operation medicines', as we call it, has begun. In the
evenings, after dinner, we go to our room and there we
wrap our jewels – diamonds, sapphires and rubies – first in
cotton wool, then linen and then we sew them into
brassières and corsets and buttons. It's quite slow and
laborious, so Trina and Countess Hendrikov are helping.
But it's nice just to feel that we're doing something useful.
Olga gets us to sing songs as we work. The guards who
accompanied Papa and Mama to Ekaterinburg have come
back. They told Colonel Kobylinsky that Prince
Dolgorukov has been put in prison.

May 2nd

'Operation medicines' completed! A letter from Marie
came today. She says that when they arrived in
Ekaterinburg they were all asked how much money they
had with them – Papa and Mama had nothing, but she
had sixteen roubles that I'd given her and she had to hand
it over. They have a tiny garden to walk in and a swing.
Nyuta has become a laundress. Marie asked if we could

bring some paints with us as she's run out. I do hope we'll be able to join them soon. Alexis is still in bed, but I think he's nearly well enough to travel.

May 4th

Colonel Kobylinsky has been sent away, which I'm very sorry and quite worried about, as I think he'd have looked after us. The soldiers here now are all Red Guards, from Ekaterinburg, and we have a new commissar called Rodionov. He's ugly and rude. He insists on a roll-call every morning.

After breakfast, my sisters and I have to line up in the drawing room and then he says to each of us – 'Are you Olga Nicolaevna?' 'Are you Anastasia Nicolaevna?' etc. Today he said, 'There are so many of you and you all look alike – how can I be expected to remember your names?' As if there were hundreds of us, not three! And he's forbidden us from locking the door of our room at night, because he says he has to be able to check on us at all times.

May 7th

I looked out of the window this afternoon and saw Gleb (he's still living in the Kornilov house) in the street so I waved to him and he bowed. Then I saw Rodionov shouting and pushing Gleb. We heard later that he's forbidden anyone to look up at our windows.

May 10th

At evening prayers yesterday, Father Alexei and the nuns were stripped and searched. Had cabbage soup and veal for luncheon and then veal again, with macaroni, for dinner. Rodionov has told us that we'll be leaving soon.

May 11th

Nagorny took a bunch of radishes and a note from Alexis to Gleb. Now Nagorny's in great trouble with Rodionov. One of the Red Guards said something insulting to Tatiana and me when we walked past him in the yard this afternoon. Tatiana gave him one of her looks and I felt myself blushing, bright red. Even though I didn't quite understand what the guard had said I just knew it was disgusting. You have to behave as if you haven't heard, but it makes you feel horribly dirty.

May 19th

We're to leave tomorrow. I shan't be sorry to leave Tobolsk, even though we don't quite know what awaits us in Ekaterinburg. But we'll be together again, which is the main thing. Very busy all day packing. Tatiana and I are going to wear the brassières and Olga a corset, with our 'medicines'. The brassières in particular are extremely heavy and you feel as though you're going to topple flat on your face.

May 20th, on board the Russia

At dinner last night, our last in the Governor's house,

Tatiana suddenly said, 'I think we should have some wine,' which is not at all like her, but which seemed like a good idea. It turned out there were just two bottles left, so they were brought up. As we were sipping and toasting each other we heard Rodionov's voice outside and we just had time to hide the bottles and our glasses under the table before he came in. He gave us a very suspicious look and said, 'Be ready to leave at 9 a.m.' He'd barely closed the door before we all began to laugh hysterically, as you do when you've nearly been caught doing something forbidden. So it was a strangely merry last dinner.

Now we're on the *Russia*, the same boat that brought us to Tobolsk, on our way to Tiumen. Nagorny had to carry Alexis on board, because he still can't walk and now they've both been locked in their cabin, even though Monsieur Gilliard tried to explain that we need to be able to visit Alexis. But my sisters and I aren't allowed to lock the door of our cabin at all. Tatiana has announced that she's not going to bed and that she's going to sit in front of the door, but as that doesn't seem fair we're going to take shifts. The soldiers on board stare at us all the time and it doesn't feel safe.

May 21st

Something horrible happened this morning. Tatiana and I were walking along the deck, on our way to the dining saloon for breakfast, when we saw two soldiers coming towards us. There wasn't much space and one of the men brushed against Tatiana – she was ahead of me – as he came past. She gave a sort of exclamation and whirled around and the man laughed. I asked her what had happened, what the matter was, and she said, 'He touched me!' She was shaking. I thought we should tell someone, but Tatiana just said, 'Who can we tell? Who's going to do anything? No, I don't want anyone to know about this, least of all Papa and Mama. Promise you won't tell.' So I promised.

May 22nd, on the train

When we got to Tiumen the *Russia* moored near a train. We got off and lined up and Rodionov read out names from a list. The suite and the servants were called onto the train first. Then the four of us. We're in a carriage on our own. It's filthy. We haven't had anything to eat today, apart from some bowls of kasha* that someone brought us for luncheon.

May 23rd, Ekaterinburg

I can't describe how happy I felt to see Papa and Mama and Marie, to embrace them, to be able to tell them everything. They hardly got any of our letters. We've been clinging to each other for most of the day. I'm going to write this properly tomorrow.

May 24th

Our train arrived at Ekaterinburg in the middle of the night. It kept being shunted backwards and forwards before we were told, at about seven in the morning, that we could get off. It was pouring with rain. Olga, Tatiana and I walked along the platform, sinking into the mud, dragging our suitcases. I was also carrying Jimmy, which didn't make it any easier, and Nagorny tried to take my suitcase, but one of the soldiers pushed him away.

We could see everyone else, still on the train – Trina smiled at us and Countess Hendrikov made the sign of the cross and Mr Gibbes gave a sort of salute. We got into drozhkies while Nagorny went back for Alexis. Now here we are in our new – I was going to write 'home', but 'prison' is more like it. There's a high wooden fence all around the house, like Tobolsk, and the windows have been painted white, which means you can't see out; it makes the light inside seem strange and ghostly, as if you're buried in a cloud. Our rooms are on the upper floor. It's called 'The House of Special Purpose'.

May 25th

Only Trup, our footman, and Kharitonov, our cook, have been allowed to come with us into 'The House of Special Purpose'. We don't know where the other servants, or Mr Gibbes, Monsieur Gilliard, Trina and the rest, have gone. We have five rooms. Papa, Mama and Alexis have one room, we girls have another, Dr Botkin is in the drawing room and the servants sleep in the kitchen and the hall. We don't have beds yet, so last night Marie gave hers to Alexis.

Our luggage, even our vanity cases, was taken away to be searched when we arrived and we haven't got it back yet. I was very pleased to see Lenka again. He's been turned into a kind of kitchen boy, which he doesn't seem to mind, but he says things are much harder here than at Tobolsk. He's normally the most cheery and obliging boy. Now he looks nervous and scared.

I had a long talk with Marie last night. She said their journey to Ekaterinburg had been very frightening – first they thought that they might drown when they were crossing the river, then their train was stopped and they found out that they were going to Ekaterinburg, not Moscow, which made Papa very worried. And of course Mama couldn't stop thinking about us, and Alexis especially, so Marie had to try and keep her spirits up. And, when they arrived in Ekaterinburg, people shouted awful things like 'Show us the Romanov parasites!' and 'Death to Nicholas the blood drinker!' She says she feels miles older after these last few weeks. I told her what had happened to Tatiana on the *Russia*.

May 27th

The commandant here is called Alexander Avdeev. He's very rough and rude and I think he drinks. He let us have our luggage back this morning. Soldiers stand guard outside our rooms with revolvers and they just barge in whenever they feel like it, without knocking. Dr Botkin has written a letter asking for Monsieur Gilliard to be sent to us, because Alexis needs him. I don't know if it'll do any good.

May 29th

There's only one bathtub for the twelve of us, so baths are rationed – two a week (Mr Gibbes would be most unhappy!). Marie helped me wash my hair this evening. Until we left Tsarskoe Selo I'd never washed my hair – Shura always did it – so I find it hard to manage on my own. At least it isn't nearly as long as it used to be. We hardly have any of the things we brought from the Alexander Palace here – our china, pictures, lamps etc. They seem to have disappeared during the journey from Tobolsk. It means this house feels very bare and unfriendly. My sisters' and my room has yellowish wallpaper, all faded and stained, four little iron beds, a small table and that's it. We've put up our icons, though.

May 30th

We're followed by soldiers even when we go to the lavatory. They stand right outside the door. This morning, as I was going in, one of them said, 'Make sure you enjoy the artwork.' Inside, on the wall, there were disgusting drawings of Mama and Our Friend. I tried to rub them off, but I couldn't. Marie says it's particularly embarrassing when you have Becker, because you know that the soldiers know and they laugh and make jokes. I'm dreading that.

June 3rd

It's terribly hot now and we swelter in our rooms as we're not allowed to open the windows. Our only breath of air is when we have our walk in the garden. It's hard on Jimmy and Joy. Alexis was carried out today and sat on a chair in the sun. Mama isn't well – she's feeling dizzy and she has a bad headache and pains in her legs. Tatiana is reading to her. We had a treat this evening – a small piece of chocolate each, the last of some bars that Aunt Ella sent a few weeks ago (there was some coffee too, which is good for Mama's headaches). Since then Papa has heard that Aunt Ella was forced to leave her abbey. I think she's a prisoner now too.

June 4th

We're very upset because Nagorny has gone. He had already had an argument with Avdeev because the soldiers had said Alexis could only have one pair of boots and Nagorny tried to explain he has to have two, in case one gets wet. Then yesterday he caught a guard stealing the gold chain, with Alexis's collection of holy images, which was hanging from his bed, so naturally he tried to stop him. He was arrested immediately. Alexis has been crying all day – now he doesn't have Monsieur Gilliard or Nagorny.

The fence around the house has been made higher, which means we can partly open some of the windows, but not so you can see out or anything. I suppose we should be grateful.

June 6th

Jimmy, who's normally the friendliest dog in the world, has

taken a great dislike to Avdeev. He growls whenever Avdeev comes anywhere near him. This morning Avdeev shouted, 'If you can't keep that dog under control I'll have him shot!' which just shows what a brute he is, but I'm petrified he means it.

June 7th

There's been a great row. While we were dressing, Tatiana knocked over Olga's bottle of Jasmine perfume (her favourite) and it spilled. Olga went absolutely berserk and kept shouting, 'That's the last perfume I'll ever have and now it's gone and it's all your fault!' Poor Tatiana burst into tears and Papa had to come and calm everyone down. He said, 'It's more important now than ever that we be patient and gentle with each other.' Now Olga is embracing Tatiana and they're both crying.

June 8th

The days feel very, very long. There are no lessons and we have hardly any exercise. We get up at eight and have morning prayers. Then there's breakfast – just black bread and tea. Then we girls help Nyuta with the housework – darning and mending clothes and sometimes laundering – which at least is an occupation. Luncheon is at two and it's always the same – soup and cutlets, sent over from the local soup kitchen, which Kharitonov heats up. We eat with the servants. At first they were very embarrassed, in fact Nyuta said it wasn't right and she couldn't eat with us, but now everyone has got used to it. There's no cloth on the table and we share five forks.

Sometimes I think of the banquets there used to be at Tsarskoe Selo, with the tables all glittering with porcelain and silver and crystal, and look at us now! In the afternoon we go into the garden for an hour – Papa has to carry Alexis out. Dinner isn't much of a meal. Today we were told that we can't have cream any more (I really think I'm getting slimmer at last). We spend the evenings knitting and doing embroidery. Papa reads – he's started *War and Peace*. Sometimes we play cards. We don't talk that much, even Alexis and me who are normally chatterboxes. It feels a bit like we're holding our breath.

June 9th

I'm worried about the guards reading this diary, so I keep it with me at all times.

June 10th, Sunday

Sunday. A priest called Father Storozhov came to say mass. One of the soldiers reported that he'd heard Mama speaking to us girls in German, which is absolute nonsense – she never speaks to us in German, mostly because our German is so hopeless. But we got a warning from Avdeev anyway. It's hotter than ever.

June 12th

After dinner the soldiers often start singing their revolutionary songs, like 'Get Cheerfully in Step Comrades', with a lot of stamping and clapping. When we heard them this evening Mama said, 'I think we should sing our own songs and drown them out.' So Olga played the piano and Mama, Tatiana, Marie and I sang hymns. You could still hear the soldiers downstairs, but it helped.

June 18th
My birthday. I'm seventeen. There's really nothing else to say.

June 19th
Today at lunch Avdeev came in – the soldiers often watch us eating – leaned over Papa, practically jabbing him in the face with his elbow, and helped himself to one of our cutlets, saying 'I think you idle rich have had quite enough'. Dr Botkin is very worried about Gleb and Tatiana – he doesn't know if they're still in Tobolsk, or whether their grandmother has been able to come and take them back to Tsarskoe Selo. Mama says we must remember how hard it is for Dr Botkin and the servants – after all they're only here because of us and they don't have their families with them. You can see a little muscle jumping under Lenka's eye, even though he's always putting up his hand to stop it.

June 22nd
Marie and I asked Avdeev if we could have a camera and of course he refused. I helped Nyuta wash Mama's hair. Nyuta had made the water too hot, so Mama snapped at her and she burst into tears. Mama's awfully bad-tempered

these days – she gets impatient with Nyuta because she's nervous and clumsy, so then she snaps at her and of course that just makes Nyuta worse.

After dinner Mama read aloud from the Bible, while we girls embroidered and Alexis made wire chains for his model ship. Papa just sat and smoked (he smokes more than ever now). I asked him how long he thought we'd be here and he said, 'I wish I could answer that, Anastasia'.

June 27th

The last few days have been terribly anxious and exhausting, all because Papa received two letters saying we should prepare to be rescued by some people who were devoted to us! We didn't know whether to believe the letters, or what we should do exactly, so Papa told us to pack just a few essential things. Last night we all stayed awake – apart from Alexis, who went to bed – fully dressed, wearing our 'medicines', but nothing happened. It was torture. I think it's worse, having the hope of being rescued and then not being, than not having the hope in the first place. I don't think anyone can help us now.

June 28th

Papa has discovered that the soldiers have been going through our big trunks, that are kept in an outhouse, and taking things. He's complained to Avdeev, but I don't suppose that'll make any difference. My sisters and I have started helping Kharitonov make bread. Kneading dough turns out to be a very satisfying activity. One of the soldiers came into the kitchen and looked quite astonished to see us at the kitchen table, covered in flour. He said, 'It's all in the wrist – let me show you,' and he gave us a demonstration. I asked him if he'd been a baker and he said he'd worked in his father's bakery when he was a boy.

It's the first time any of the soldiers has spoken to us in a friendly way. My first loaf was distinctly heavy, but Papa and Mama declared it delicious. Poor Dr Botkin has broken his glasses – he's practically blind without them and Avdeev won't let him have new ones.

July 1st

When we were sitting together in the drawing room last night Avdeev came in with some of his guards. You could tell they were drunk. Avdeev said, 'We fancy some music – we'd like one of you young ladies to play for us.' We all froze and no one said anything for a minute. Then Olga looked at Mama and Mama nodded to her and said quietly, 'It's all right, Olga, just play them something.' So Olga went and sat at the piano and played. You could see how much she hated it by the way she sat, all stiff, but she got through her piece with hardly any mistakes, which I couldn't have done for anything. When she'd finished the soldiers applauded and cheered in a sarcastic kind of way and then they left, thankfully. Olga burst into tears and we all hugged her.

July 2nd

Spent the morning in the kitchen with Kharitonov,

making bread. I'd probably never have talked to Kharitonov if we hadn't ended up all together like this. He has a very mournful expression and he hardly ever smiles, but when you talk to him you realise what a kind man he is. He told me he'd never particularly wanted to be a cook, but he'd grown up in Tsarskoe Selo and his mother had taught him a bit, and so when his father died and he had to get a job, he applied to be a kitchen boy at the Alexander Palace. He doesn't think he's much good at cooking. I said, 'Well, I bet you wish now you'd gone to work for some other family.' And he looked very serious and said that it was an honour to serve us in any way he could and that he'd willingly die for Papa (he insists on still calling him the Tsar). I had to leave the room then because I could feel tears pricking. It is a comfort, though, to know that not everyone hates us.

July 4th

Avdeev and his soldiers have been replaced. There's a new commandant, called Jacob Yurovsky and new guards. We didn't like the old guards, but at least some of them had started to seem almost friendly. These new ones have very hard, unsmiling faces. They don't talk to us. They don't even look at us. Still, Yurovsky apologised to Papa about the stealing from our luggage and said he would put a stop to it.

July 5th

Yurovsky has made a list of all our valuables (not our

medicines) and this afternoon he put them in a casket, sealed it and gave it to us. He's also putting a lock on the door of the outhouse where our trunks are kept. So perhaps he means well by us. He's certainly not drunk or rude. There's something awfully cold about him though and his expression never changes when he talks. He looks cruel in fact.

July 6th

While I was sorting through the laundry with Nyuta this morning she suddenly started to cry and said, 'Oh Anastasia Nicolaevna, I'm so afraid that these new men have come to kill us.' I had to say that of course that wasn't going to happen and no one wanted to kill us, etc. But afterwards I felt quite sick and I realised that I've never actually let myself think that we might die here.

July 8th

Last night I admitted to Marie that I feel very scared and she said she feels exactly the same. I think we all do. Olga hardly speaks and often you find her in tears, and Alexis is so pale and thin and quiet that sometimes, when he's lying on his bed or the couch fiddling with his model ship, you forget he's there at all. Tatiana is the bravest of us. She says we have to be strong for Papa and Mama and she's right.

Yurovsky has ordered that a heavy grill be fastened over the one drawing room window that we're allowed to open. Dr Botkin has found out that he and his guards belong to the Bolshevik Secret Police. I'm afraid that can only be bad.

July 9th

The soles of my shoes are completely worn through, so this morning I went to find Yurovsky, to ask if I could have a look through our trunks, for another pair. He was sitting at the desk in the guard room, smoking and looking out of the window. When I'd explained about the shoes he looked straight at me and said, 'I think you'll find the shoes you have will last you long enough,' and then he just stubbed out his cigarette and walked out of the room. I've noticed that he never seems to blink.

July 11th

Jimmy won't leave my side for a second these days, not even to run in the garden.

July 13th

Lenka has been sent away. We couldn't understand why, so Tatiana went to ask Yurovsky. He told her that Lenka's uncle has arrived in Ekaterinburg and he's gone to meet him and he didn't know when he'd be back. It does seem strange – Lenka never mentioned that he even had an uncle and why didn't he say goodbye?

July 14th

Father Storozhov came to conduct a service. He looked at us so kindly and sadly – it was unbearable. Marie and

Olga cried, all the way through. It's funny, I used to be quite proud of the fact that I hardly ever cried and now hardly a day goes by when I *don't* cry. And if it's not me it's someone else.

July 16th

A beautiful sunny day. Yurovsky brought some eggs for Alexis. We walked in the garden in the afternoon while Alexis sat in the sun. Now, after dinner, Olga is reading aloud from the Bible, Tatiana and Marie are sewing and Papa and Mama are playing bezique.

This is the last entry in Anastasia's diary. At 2 a.m. on July 17th, Yurovsky woke Dr Botkin and ordered him to rouse the rest of the prisoners. They were told that they were being moved into the basement because of unrest in the town. The Tsar, carrying Alexis, came down the stairs first, followed by the Tsarina and her daughters, with Dr Botkin, Nyuta, Trup and Kharitonov bringing up the rear. Anastasia carried her spaniel, Jimmy.

Nobody spoke. In the cramped basement room the Tsar asked for two chairs, for his wife and Alexis. The others stood behind them, against the wall. Yurovsky entered the room with an execution squad of eleven men and announced, 'I've received orders to shoot you.' The Tsar just had time to say, 'What? What?' and to turn towards his family before the firing began and the room filled with black smoke and the sound of screams.

When it stopped, after several minutes of bullets ricocheting off the walls, Alexis and Anastasia were found to be still alive. Yurovsky shot Alexis in the head. One of the executioners stood on Anastasia's arms and stabbed her repeatedly with a bayonet. Jimmy had his head crushed with a rifle butt. The bodies were then loaded onto a lorry and dumped in a mineshaft. The next day they were removed, disfigured with sulphuric acid and buried in shallow graves. The sole survivor of the massacre was Joy, Alexis's spaniel, who was found wandering in the garden of 'The House of Special Purpose' by officers of the White Army, which liberated Ekaterinburg from the Bolsheviks eight days later.

Glossary

Becker/Engineer-mechanic – code words for period
Drozhky – carriage
Duma – parliament
Iconostasis – screen made from icons
Kasha – buckwheat
Kulich – Easter cake
Mors – drink made from cranberries
Paskha – Easter cheesecake
Pirozhki – stuffed pastries
Tarantass – peasant cart
Te Deum – psalm
Troika – sleigh drawn by three horses
Zakouski – appetisers

Acknowledgments

I would like to thank Pots and Ivan Samarine for giving me a glimpse of Russia, Claudia FitzHerbert and Nicole Bellamy for their comments and suggestions, and all at Short Books.

Author Biography
Kate Hubbard is the author of *A Material Girl: Bess of Hardwick* (Short Books, 2001), *WHO WAS… Charlotte Brontë* and *WHO WAS… Queen Victoria* from the Short Books children's historical biography series. She lives in London and Dorset.